SILVER BIRD

Sam Gibbons was a tomboy, through and through. Though her wealthy Boston family tried in vain to turn her into a lady, she was eager to explore and lead a life of adventure, rather than stagnate in the stultifying tea-and-cake circle of respectable society. Then she read about the Wright Brothers, Wilbur and Orville, and her life would change for ever. Buying her own aeroplane, she headed out into the Wild West . . .

BEN RAY

SILVER BIRD

Complete and Unabridged

LINFORD
Leicester

First published in Great Britain in 2018 by
Robert Hale
an imprint of The Crowood Press
Wiltshire

First Linford Edition
published 2022
by arrangement with The Crowood Press
Wiltshire

A catalogue record for this book is available
from the British Library.

ISBN 978–1–4448–4875–5

Published by
Ulverscroft Limited
Anstey, Leicestershire

Printed and bound in Great Britain by
TJ Books Ltd., Padstow, Cornwall

This book is printed on acid-free paper

1

'I'm gettin' sick to death o' beans and bacon,' growled Seth Watson as he flung the unfinished contents of his heavy tin plate into the camp-fire.

'There ain't no need fer that. I ain't cookin' jus' fer you to toss it into the fire!' His long-time partner Jacob Merlin was the cook and chief bottle-washer of the duo.

'Jesus! What I wouldn't give for a thick, juicy, steak and some o' them fine potaters, jus' a-swimmin' in the juices.' Seth smacked his lips together, belched, then farted. 'Damn beans!'

The two were heading back to Tomahawk Creek, their hometown, from a ramrodding trip to Fort Benson. Fewer cattle were being driven these days as the railroad was slowly, but surely, opening up the West, and putting the cowboys out of business.

The journey had been eventful. A

stampede or two. A half-hearted attack by some hungry savages, so skinny and scrawny that the cowboys had killed a steer and left it for them to find. Then the women. After two months in the saddle, aching backs, dust, cattle, and beans, the warmth of a woman's body, even though bought and paid for, for the night, was a welcome relief, as well as a release of trail tension.

Seth and Jacob knew they were the last of a dying breed. They were no longer feared by the townsfolk of any town in the West they visited or passed through with the cattle. The law was established in most parts now, the army on hand at the slightest provocation.

If you got drunk and disorderly, you went to jail for the night and had to pay a hefty fine to get out again. You couldn't even enter a saloon or eating house without having first visited the barber for a shave and a bath, as well as a fresh change of clothes.

No, things in the tame West were changing, and Seth and Jacob knew that, sooner or later, they'd have to change too.

Eating over, they stoked up the campfire and rolled over in their blankets. The night would be cold, but they were used to that. Except nowadays, the cold seemed to stay in their bones for a little longer in the mornings, the stiffness, after a night out in the open, sleeping on the ground, would take more than a couple of hours to disappear.

The night sky, filled with shimmering stars, was clear. The moon, full tonight, lit up the prairie with a ghostly, bluish light that made both men seem pale and drawn. The only sounds to be heard were the gentle rustle of the trees, maybe a coyote or two, far away baying at the moon. Normal sounds for two old-timers. They fell into a deep sleep.

★ ★ ★

'What in tarnation was that?' Seth tried to sit bolt upright from under his blanket, but his muscles had grown stiff, and all he managed to do was lift his head off the saddle-bag it was resting on.

'Goddamn, it's an earthquake!' Jacob, managing to extricate himself from the tangled blanket, jumped up, and stared at the trees, the rocks, and the sky in turn, looking for some sign of an earthquake.

'T'ain't no earthquake. The ground ain't movin',' Seth said.

'Then what in the hell-of-whores is it,' Jacob spat out, standing rock still.

The noise had, by now, grown softer, it seemed to be moving away from them. Then, as quickly as it had come, it was gone.

'Ain't no railroad hereabouts,' muttered Seth, already settling back to sleep.

'Nope. There ain't no railroads, and that weren't no train engine, neither.' Jacob was still standing, trying to pick up the sound again.

'Well, for God's sake, git back to sleep. Whatever it was, it ain't no more,' Seth growled, yawning.

Jacob rolled himself up in his blanket, kicked at the camp-fire, sending sparks up into the sky, looked around one last time, then flopped back on the ground again and fell asleep.

Although neither man owned a time-piece, they were both convinced that they'd only slept for another hour or two at the most, when the sound came thundering through their brains to wake them up again.

This time, Seth managed to stand, stamping his left leg hard on the ground to get rid of the pins and needles in his foot. 'God-blast-it-to-hell-an'-back.'

Jacob wasn't sure if Seth was shouting at the noise, or his left foot. 'Ain't no train engine.'

'I damn well know it ain't no train engine,' Seth spluttered. He went for his faithful old Colt, which he always kept under his saddle-bag when he slept.

'What in tarnation you gonna do with that?' Seth asked.

'If'n it comes round these parts agin, I'm a gonna shoot it to hell, then maybe we'll get some sleep around here.' Seth, pins and needles now abating slightly, starting limping round the campsite looking for whatever it was that was making the noise.

'Could be one o' them horseless thingamyjigs I heard about,' Jacob offered, adding more kindling to the dying camp-fire.

'Horseless? What d'ya mean, horseless?' Seth yelled. 'I ain't never heard of no such thing. What is it, a mule?'

'No, it's one o' them auto-mobiles. Heared they had 'em back east. Carries four people, 'parently.' Jacob reached into his shirt pocket and started to roll a smoke.

'What in hell do they want a horseless for?' Seth settled his Colt back in his holster and sat in front of the camp-fire warming his hands.

Jacob lit his cigarette, then coughed. He coughed for a long time.

Seth looked over to his old partner, 'Enjoying that, huh?'

'First one's the best,' Jacob replied, coughing some more.

'So what do they want with a horseless?'

Seth repeated.

'It ain't called a horseless, it's called an automobile, it runs on wheels, like a carriage, 'cept there ain't no horse pulling it. Seems like there's a engine, or somethin' that drives it along.' Jacob stacked the coffee pot on the embers of the fire, heating up last night's brew.

'Don't make no sense to me,' Seth answered.

'O' course it don't make no sense to you, you're just a lump o' horse-shit cowboy. Bet you don't even know how them there train engines work?' Jacob coughed, spat, then shook the coffee pot.

'Sure as hell I do,' Seth was indignant. 'Runs on them railroad tracks, pulling folks along.'

'I didn't ask yer what it ran on, I asked yer how it ran?' Jacob was enjoying riling his old partner.

'How in the hell am I supposed to know that?' Seth yelled. 'I ain't no railroad worker, am I?

'Knew you didn't know. Just knew it.'

Jacob drew on his cigarette and coughed again.

The sun was higher in the sky by now and both men knew that further sleep was impossible.

'So come on smart-ass, how do it work, then?' Seth was trying to call his bluff.

'Steam. Simple as that. Steam.' Jacob smiled in triumph.

'What? You 'spect me ta believe that? You're madder than a bull in heat.' Seth reached for the coffee pot, forgot to wrap a rag on the handle, and dropped it on the fire. 'Goddamn. Goddamn. Goddamn!'

'Well done, now we ain't got no coffee and you put the fire out.' Jacob was busy trying to save what little there was left of the camp-fire.

'Still don't believe in no steam driving no train engine,' Seth was unrepentant.

'Well, fer you're information, it ain't called no train engine, it's called a steam engine, smart-ass, what ya got to say to that!'

Before Seth could remonstrate further, the noise came back, loud and clear and close.

Seth leapt to his feet, went for his Colt, pulled it out of the holster and dropped it on the ground. The bullet missed Jacob by no more than a hair's breadth.

'Jesus H. Christ. Ya damn well near blew ma brains out.' Jacob flopped backwards on to his bedroll, feeling himself for a wound or blood, or anything.

'Damn safety catch needs fixin',' Seth groped around for the gun.

'Ya bin sayin' that practically since I've known ya,' Jacob said, getting back on his feet.

The noise seemed very close, but still they couldn't see anything. Then there came a grating sound, like the sound of twisted metal.

Both men looked at each other. They kept very still and quiet.

'Seems to be comin' from behind those trees, over yonder.' Jacob pointed to his left. 'You circle around to the right, I'll cut through to the left. Don't shoot at anything until you're sure it ain't me.'

'Don't you start a-givin' me orders, you ain't no boss o' mine.' Seth whispered hoarsely.

'Well suit yerself then. I'm goin' round to the left and see what the hell that was.'

With that, Jacob crept off into the half-light of dawn. Seth stood for a while, then said to himself, *If he's goin' round that way, I guess I'll circle round the other way.* Yeah, that makes sense to me, all right. And with that, he did exactly as his partner had asked.

Both men, although old, knew how to tread softly, their beer-bellies were the only things that stopped them crawling, Indian-style, towards their quarry. Soon, both Seth and Jacob saw at last what had been making all the din. There, resting on what appeared to be its nose, was the strangest contraption either man had ever seen.

It seemed to be made of some sort of cloth and string, and had two wheels on the bottom of it, one of which was bent and the axle twisted. On top, there was a person, unconscious, it seemed, perched inside the thing.

Seth and Jacob moved slowly forward, guns drawn. 'Don't go pointin' that thing at me, or anywhere near me,' Jacob whispered.

'You jus' look to yerself. Let's see what kinda un-Godly contraption this is, and what in the hell is in it,' Seth replied.

At that moment, a low groan wafted over the air. Whoever, or whatever, was in the contraption, was coming round.

2

The small war-party, at least that's how the Indians liked to think of themselves, had been following the thing for hours. More intrigued than frightened. They had followed the sound across the prairie, not seeing it, not finding any tracks. As the sound changed direction, so did the war-party. The braves were excited, as well as a little apprehensive. Whatever they had been following, left no tracks. So it had to be supernatural. Perhaps even Manitou himself. At last, the genocide that had been performed on the Indian race was to be avenged. The God of Gods had arrived, just in time to save them. They, too, heard the crashing sounds, albeit distantly. Their acute hearing and sense of direction overcoming their lack of sight due to the half-light. They rode on in silence. Their ponies, sensing the warriors' excitement, hardly made a sound as their unshod hoofs raced across the prairie grass.

Their leader raised his right arm in the air to signal a halt, and the war-party reined in their ponies and listened. Silence.

They waited but the silence grew ominous. Slowly the ponies cantered on. The Indian leader raised his arm once more, sniffing the breeze. Smoke. He could smell a faint but unmistakable trace of smoke. Again they moved on, slower this time, barely making any sound. Then, as one, they all slid from their mounts and crouched in the half-light.

Taking their ponies into a small copse, the Indians spread out and waited. In the silence they all winced as one of their party, hunger getting the better of him, belched and the rumbling noise his stomach made they were sure, could be heard for miles.

The sound of horses' hoofs broke their concentration. One, two, three, four riders, moving fast. The Indians turned, for this new threat was behind them. They felt trapped. What they had been following was in front of them, now this. Quickly they remounted their ponies and rode deeper into the copse.

Instinctively, they drew their weapons, bows, knives, tomahawks, and waited. Their rifles had been confiscated at the Reservation, along with their pride. But these young braves, too young to have fought in the last great battles against the white man, were adept with their traditional tools of warfare, or at least, they hoped they were.

★ ★ ★

James Benson was a twenty-two-year-old ranch hand on a smallholding in the middle of nowhere. At six feet three inches tall, broad shouldered and with a mop of blond hair, he was a striking figure of a man.

His piercing blue eyes always seemed to be laughing.

But James was getting bored. Mild mannered and even tempered, James didn't socialize much, if at all. It didn't seem worth the effort of riding into the one-horse town that was a day's ride away and Doug Hendricks, the owner of the smallholding, drove the buckboard into town once a month to get supplies. He sold a few vegetables and sometimes butchered a steer to sell the meat.

It meant a stay-over for James, which meant he'd get drunk and return the next day with most of the supplies he went in for. There was always something he forgot, even though Doug had written a list for him every month. He either forgot to take it, or left it in his back pocket and forgot to give it to the sutler's storekeeper.

James had had plenty of time to think about his future. His parents had died, the doc said cholera, and he had left the family home, not being able to face living there.

He'd chanced upon Doug on a trail, standing beside a buckboard with a missing wheel.

Fortunately, the buckboard was empty,

Doug being on his way to town, and the wheel wasn't damaged.

'Need a hand there, mister?' James asked.

'Sure could do with some help here, mister,' Doug replied.

Doug dismounted and got James to get the wheel.

When the wheel was in position, Doug lifted up the buckboard. 'Tell me when it's high enough,' Doug said.

'It's fine where it is,' James replied and slid the wheel back on to the axle.

Doug gently lowered the buckboard and began looking for a suitable cotter pin.

'You got a mallet?' James asked.

'Sure have.' Doug reached under the driver's seat and handed it to James, who hammered the piece of wood into position.

'How far's the nearest town?' asked James.

'No more'n five miles,' Doug said.

'Well, if you take it easy you'll be OK. But you need to get to a wheelwright and get a proper pin there,' James said.

'Mighty obliged, mister. Name's Doug Hendricks. Got a small place back a few miles. You ain't lookin' for work are you?' he asked.

'Could be,' James replied. My name's James Benson. What you got in mind?'

'I got a small herd, fifty or so, and a remuda of ten horses, so it's mainly keeping an eye on them. Getting too old for me most days, it's all I can do to plant seeds for food.'

'Guess I can handle that,' James said.

Doug raised his hand to shake on it, and James lowered his.

'Let's get to town,' Doug said, 'I got me a raging thirst,' he grinned and climbed aboard his buckboard.

★ ★ ★

That had been a year ago and James needed to move on.

Doug was genuinely sorry to see him go but, deep down, he knew this was no life for a young man.

17

'I packed some vittles for your journey,' Doug said, not looking into James's eyes. 'You take care now, ya hear?'

'I will Doug, and thanks for everything.'

James wheeled his mount round and rode away. He didn't look back once.

* * *

James had been heading westwards for the first three weeks, living off the land to eke out his rations.

It was dusk and he was looking for a decent place to camp for the night when he smelled smoke.

More than smoke. He smelled coffee.

Following his nose he walked his animal slowly, already his mouth was watering.

'Hello the camp,' James called out.

He saw three men seated round the fire. They all drew their guns and moved out of the light.

'Show yourself, mister,' a voice called out.

James raised his hands, guiding his

horse with his knees.

'Hold it there,' a different voice this time.

James halted his mount, his hands still raised high above his head.

A man approached him, his handgun pointing at James's chest.

'Throw your gun down,' the man ordered.

'If'n it's all the same to you, I'd rather toss it to you. I just cleaned and oiled it.'

The man thought for a second or two, then: 'OK, thumb and forefinger only and hold it by the grip. Any movement and I shoot. Understand?'

'Understood,' James replied. Slowly he lowered his right hand and did as he was ordered, he pulled the Colt from its holster and tossed it to the man, who deftly caught it.

'Now you can dismount,' the man said.

James dismounted and stretched his aching back. Then reached for his canteen. Taking off his Stetson, he filled the hat with water and held it for his horse.

'That coffee sure smells good,' James said.

'Help yourself, stranger.' Another man appeared from the other side of the fire.

'Name's James.'

'Good to meet you James, I'm Lewis, this here's Hank and yonder is Brad.'

'I don't believe it! James grinned. 'I'm James Benson. We went to school together in Mesa Verde.'

The three men rushed forward to shake hands.

'What brings you out this way?' Lewis asked.

'Lookin' for work. Seems it's mighty scarce in these parts.'

'Sure is, we're doin' the same thing. Seems the railroad is putting us out to pasture.' Hank said and squatted in front of the fire, pouring a cup of coffee.

'There's a town about a day's ride from here. We're aiming to camp here tonight and set out at first light. You're welcome to join us. I'm afraid we ain't got no food to offer you, though.'

'I got beans an' some bread that's seen

better days, and there's some bacon, but you're welcome to share it,' James said.

'That's mighty neighbourly of you, James. We ain't eaten today.' Hank reached into a saddle-bag and produced a large pot.

'This oughta do,' he said as his stomach rumbled.

Some thirty minutes later, the camp went silent as the men ate.

⋆ ⋆ ⋆

Just over a mile behind the four men, three other men had set up camp, also on their way to town, known as Dry Gulch.

But their reason for going there was not to look for work.

3

At first light, the two sets of travellers set off. It didn't take the following group long to spot the riders ahead.

'What d'you think, Bill,' Burt asked. 'Shall we catch 'em up?

'Don't see why not, they could be useful when we get to town,' Bill answered. 'But let them think there's just the three of us, OK?'

'OK. Let's speed it up a little,' Chas said and dug his heels into his mount's flanks.

'Not too fast,' Bill cautioned, 'we don't want to scare them off or start a gunfight.'

Chas reined in and settled for a gentle trot, still gaining on the men ahead.

'Hello, ahead!' Bill called out.

James reined in and turned around, his Colt already drawn.

Lewis, Hank and Brad followed suit, but they held their Winchesters, pointed at the ground.

'You heading for Dry Gulch?' Bill asked.

'What's it to you where we're heading,' James replied.

'Just that we're headed that way too, and thought we might be able to join forces. There's safety in numbers,' Bill said, still walking his horse forward.

'What's your business in Dry Gulch?' James asked.

'We got some papers to sign at the bank. Bought ourselves some land, we aim to start a horse ranch,' Bill replied.

'Sounds like a good idea,' James said. 'We bin lookin' for work, but there ain't none around no more,' he added.

'Ain't that the truth,' Bill said. 'Seems cowboys are a dying breed. Railroads have taken over droving, two or three days loading steers, instead of two or three months drivin' a herd.'

'The world sure is changing,' James agreed. 'You're welcome to ride the trail with us. Not sure where we'll go after Dry Gulch. But there must be some work — someplace.'

* * *

The seven riders reached the outskirts of Dry Gulch just as dusk was falling. Soon it would be dark.

'Guess we'd better find somewhere's to camp,' James said.

'You as broke as we are?' Bill asked, but it was more of a statement.

'We got enough for breakfast, and that's about it,' James said.

'Same here,' Bill replied. 'Come on, let's find a good site to camp.'

James nodded his agreement.

It didn't take long for the men to find a suitable campsite. A hollow, with large rocks on the town side, so even their mounts were hidden from view.

Dismounting, the men stretched their aching muscles, then ground-hitched their animals. There was grass aplenty, so the animals were content. Even more so when their saddles were removed.

The men unwrapped their bed

rolls — there was no chance of lighting a fire — and settled down, trying to sleep.

★ ★ ★

The sun had been up for quite some time before the men woke up, feeling the warmth on their faces.

James took out his Hunter and checked the time.

It was 8 a.m.

'Some sort of eatery should be open by now,' James stated.

'Let's get to it,' Chas said, grabbing his saddle.

'How much money we got?' Bill asked.

'I got three dollars and some change,' James said.

'We got four dollars between us,' Bill said.

Lewis, Hank and Brad coughed up another nine dollars.

'Hell! We got more'n enough for a slap-up breakfast.'

Within five minutes, the men had saddled up and were heading towards

25

Dry Gulch.

'I reckon we should split up afore we hit town,' Bill said as he rode beside James. 'Might seem a tad strange, seven strangers riding into town,' he added.

James thought about this for a while. It made sense, but inexplicably it also made James suspicious. 'OK,' he agreed eventually. 'I guess it makes sense. You wanna go in first?'

'As long as you don't mind. Wait for say, thirty minutes and then come on in. You'll see our horses. OK?'

'OK,' James replied, but everything was not OK.

He watched as the three men rode off down the trail at a steady trot.

Lewis, Hank and Brad rode up to James. 'What's going on?' Brad asked.

'I'm not sure,' James replied. 'Bill suggested we split up as he thought it would draw attention if seven strangers rode into town.'

'Makes sense,' Hank said. 'You know what these small town folk are like. What they don't know they make up,' he laughed.

'That's as maybe. I wonder what their business is with a small town bank?' James was thinking out loud.

'They told us,' Hank said.

'Yeah, they did. But I think we should keep our eyes open. They seem a mite *too* friendly, if you ask me.' James dismounted and rolled a quirly. His partners followed suit.

'How long we gotta wait?' Lewis asked.

'Bill said thirty minutes, but I reckon I finish my smoke, then we ride in. That OK with you boys?' James said.

All three men nodded their assent. 'Sooner the better,' Lewis said.

Stubbing out their cigarettes, they mounted up and headed for Dry Gulch.

★ ★ ★

'Where in the hell are the rest of the boys?' Chas asked.

'Beats me. They should have arrived here at dawn,' Bill replied.

'So what do we do now?' Burt said

between mouthfuls of ham, steak and eggs.

'We go ahead as planned. The bank opens at 9 a.m. sharp, that's five minutes from now. There ain't no queue outside an' I bin watching the staff arrive for the past ten minutes. Should be easy pickings, boys.'

Chas wasn't convinced. 'How many guards are there? How many staff? We got enough ammo?'

'I saw one guard, an old-timer by the look of him. I also saw four staff members and a rather fat man, who I assume is the manager as he unlocked the bank's front door. Happy?'

Chas nodded.

'We can take 'em easy,' said Bill, smiling as he finished his breakfast.

Draining the last of the coffee, he paid the bill and stood.

'I ain't finished yet,' Chas complained.

'In a few minutes you'll be able to eat like a king,' Bill said. 'So leaving a little bit of steak ain't no big deal. Let's move *now*!' Reluctantly, Chas crammed the last of the steak into his mouth and was tempted to take the rest of the ham with him, but he followed Bill and Burt.

They walked casually across the main street and headed for the bank.

Chas was still chewing as he drew his Colt and entered the building.

The three men calmly walked to the cash counter and pointed their guns at the cashiers.

'Hand over the money,' Bill said.

'We can't,' one of the cashiers said. The safe doesn't open 'til 9.30. It's on a time lock.'

'A *what*?' Bill said.

'It's a lock that automatically opens the vault and there's nothing we can do to change the time it opens. It can only be done by the makers and they're based in Boston.'

'You got ten seconds to open that safe,' Bill grated.

'I'm telling you, mister, it can't be done, honest.'

A shot rang out.

At first Bill thought one of his men

had fired it but, as he turned round he saw the ancient guard cocking his pistol, ready to fire again.

Bill didn't give him the chance.

Bill pulled the trigger and the slug entered the old man's head, blowing the back of it out in a mass of bone, brain and flesh.

The old man was rocked back on his feet, but whether by chance or whether it was deliberate, he loosed off a final shot that caught Chas in the foot.

'Goddamn!' Chas cried out. 'He damn near shot my foot off.' In his anger, he pumped five shots into the already dead guard.

'We better vamoose,' Bill said. Those shots are bound to draw a crowd. Let's move.'

★ ★ ★

After a twenty-minute gallop, James and his partners reached the outskirts of Dry Gulch. That's when they heard the gunshots.

James held up his arm to halt the riders. 'Just as I thought,' he said.

'The *business* at the bank was robbing it!'

'We better vamoose afore we get involved,' Lewis said.

They turned their mounts and headed back down the trail. About a mile back they'd seen a fork in the trail and that's where they headed.

On reaching the fork, they wheeled their mounts around and set off at a gallop, heading towards the plains.

They kept their pace up for as long as their mounts could keep going. But, eventually, they had to rein in and walk the sweat-coated animals.

'Reckon we're some twenty miles from Dry Gulch.' Lewis said. 'I can't see signs of a posse. We'll rest the horses, let them get their breath back, then take it easy for a while.'

After thirty minutes, the four men had fed and watered their horses and mounted up. Ahead they could see what looked like a group of shacks, but as they got closer they could see it was a small mining camp — complete with a saloon.

All around, all they could see was grass and in the far distance a small copse of trees. Where there were trees, there was usually water to be had.

'Let's head for those trees,' Hank said. 'It'll give us some shelter from the sun.'

'Let's head for the camp first,' James said. 'I could do with a beer. That OK with you fellas?'

'Sure, why not,' Lewis spoke for them all.

They rode into the camp and hitched their horses to the rail outside the saloon, which turned out to be a large tent.

They walked up to the makeshift counter, which was four beer barrels and a plank placed on top.

'What'll it be, gents?' the barkeep asked.

'Four beers, cold as you can,' James said.

'Comin' right up,' the barkeep said.

James took a look round the saloon while he waited for his beer. There were maybe ten or fifteen men sitting and another ten standing around a table, where an old-timer was relating a story. James picked up his beer and edged closer to hear what was going on.

'Thanks for the beer, Charlie,' Henry, the storyteller said. 'Now, where was I?'

'You was sayin' they had a hearty breakfast,' Charlie said.

'They sure did,' Henry said and took a mighty gulp of his beer. Wiping his beard, he continued: 'I watched 'em leave and walk across Main, casual as you like. One of 'em was still eatin'.

'Anyways, they headed for the bank. I thought it a bit strange as everybody knows that safe don't unlock itself 'til nine-thirty. They was a half hour too early.

'It was quiet for a time, then the shootin' started. I guessed ol' Harry took a pot at them. He's as blind as a bat. How he got that job I'll never know. Anyways, the shootin' didn't last long. I heard three maybe four shots, then them three robbers came hobblin' outta the bank, saddled up and rode like the wind.'

'Anyone go after 'em?' Charlie asked.

'Hell no, they got clean away. I ran as fast as these ol' legs would carry me an' inside the bank I saw ol' Harry, crumpled on the floor.

'The back of his head was missing. He never stood a chance.' Henry paused. 'He musta hit at least one of 'em as there was blood on the floor well away from Harry's body.

'The stupid fools didn't have a clue about robbin' a bank. They had arrived in Dry Gulch the day after the mining wages had been paid out. They entered the bank at exactly 9.00 a.m. There were no customers there waiting to withdraw, the safe was never opened until 9.30 a.m, so there wasn't even any cash behind the counter.'

It was Luther Barns who spoke next. He was one of the junior tellers and had been sent home as the bank would remain closed for the rest of the day.

'What there was, was that very officious guard, Ol' Harry, armed with a rifle, who sneaked up behind them, sending a slug into one of the outlaws.

'Harry struggled to cock the rifle for another shot, but he didn't stand a chance.

'As Harry hit the floor his rifle loosed off a slug and it hit the foot of another outlaw.'

Henry took over again: 'They ran. And, despite their wounds, managed to mount up and ride as if the Devil was chasing them.'

The story-telling ended and the men began to drift away. James related the tale to his new friends. 'Doubtless, it'll be embellished as time goes on.'

All conversation ceased abruptly as a strange noise filled the air.

'What the hell . . . ' James began, but pandemonium had broken out as the noise grew louder and seemed to come from everywhere at the same time.

James looked towards the heavens just as the clouds parted momentarily, and could hardly believe his eyes.

For a split second he saw what looked

like a giant silver bird. No sooner had he blinked than it disappeared back into the clouds.

The noise grew fainter and James urged his partners to leave the saloon and mount up, pronto!

'What's up, James?' Lewis said.

'I don't know, but I sure saw something up there.' He pointed skywards. 'It was heading west.'

'What the hell was it?' Hank asked.

'I ain't got a clue,' James replied, 'but I sure aim to find out.'

4

James seemed to have become their leader.

Hank, the tallest of the four, was sallow-complexioned, with long black hair and dark brown eyes. He was the joker and could see the funny side of practically anything.

Lewis, the youngest at just eighteen, also looked the eldest. His weather-hardened face, the result of years of manual labour on his stepfather's ranch, told his life story. After his father was killed by Mexican bandits, his mother remarried. Lewis and his stepfather did not get on. Neither did he get on with his stepbrother and sister, so he made up his mind to leave and see where the trail led him.

And finally, there was Brad, the quiet one of the group. Half Mexican, half American, he had lost both his parents in a supposed Indian raid that turned out to be Mexicans hired by the railroad company. His father would not sell his homestead, or allow the railroad to cross it, so they killed him, took over the land and ran the railroad across it anyhow.

They pulled to a halt just outside the same copse that was hiding the Indian party, listening.

'Don't seem to hear nothin',' James said.

'It came this way, I'm sure it did,' said Lewis. Of all of them, it was Lewis who was the most excited. He hadn't thought of fame or fortune when they started following the noise, his immediate reaction was that something from outer space had come down to Earth, and he wanted to be the first one to see it.

'Let's make camp and have some chow, my belly thinks my throat's been cut.' Hank was always ready to eat.

'Hell, it can't be far away, let's just scout around for a bit,' Lewis could hardly contain himself.

'Well, let's make camp first. We'll wait for daylight, then we can have a good look-see.' James had made his mind up, so it was useless for Lewis to argue.

★ ★ ★

Silently, the Indian party crept through the undergrowth to catch a glimpse of whoever had just arrived. One Indian had stayed with the ponies, the other two, war paint glistening in the blue glow, hardly dared breathe as they made their way towards the far side of the copse.

As they neared the tree line, they came to a halt and, peering through the brush, caught sight of the four riders, one of whom was relieving himself too close for comfort.

Satisfied that the four riders were unaware of their presence, they crawled back to the horses.

James had been dying to go to the toilet for about the past four hours but riding hard, and being the leader, it would have meant a loss of face, to him, to pull up and empty both bowel and bladder. Besides, on the prairie there was no shelter, no privacy.

He had just pulled his trousers back up when there was a blast of noise that nearly made him fall over.

The horses, who had been quietly grazing, relieved to rest at last after the night's ride, shied and whinnied. He also heard other horses doing the same thing.

'Quick, into the trees,' he shouted to his companions.

Moving like a herd of buffalo, and making as much noise, they all jumped into the undergrowth and, breathing heavily, kept watch.

As the Indians neared their own ponies, they too heard the noise. Manitou was indeed near. They quickly quieted their mounts and, silently, kept watch.

Nearby, Seth and Jacob, in their anxiety, both fell to the ground. Seth's revolver let fly with a bullet as he hit the ground.

'Goddamn-you-to-hell,' Jacob hoarsely whispered, 'Get that damn gun fixed.'

'Jus' keep yer head down and yer mouth closed, I was close to peeing ma pants then.'

In front of the two men, the figure in the silver carriage, was trying to start up the engine, but without any success. After one last tug, the figure fell to the floor and didn't move.

Seth and Jacob stayed right where they were for another couple of minutes, then they stood and cautiously approached the fallen figure.

5

Seth and Jacob knelt beside the prostrate figure. They looked down, then at each other.

'Damned if it ain't a woman!' Seth uttered in disbelief.

Gently, they lifted the inert body and carried it back to the campsite.

'How in the hell did she get out here?' Jacob stood scratching his head.

Seth removed the leather helmet and goggles and gazed at the woman. She was beautiful. Her long auburn hair cascaded down her shoulders, her complexion was flawless.

Jacob just stood staring at her rich, full, vermillion lips, 'She's the most beautiful female I've seen in a long time.'

'You just keep a hold of yourself, you damn old coot,' Seth said as he heaped more kindling on the fire. We'd better get her coat off, and tend that wound on her forehead before she bleeds to death.'

Jacob went to his horse, removed the canteen from the pommel and brought it over to Seth. 'Here, mop her brow with this.' He handed the canteen to Seth, who tore a strip of cloth, poured water on it, and began dabbing at the woman's forehead.

'Goddamn it, you ain't washing no steer, take care, you damned ol' fool!' Jacob grabbed the cloth and gently dabbed at the wound.

The woman moved, and a low moan escaped her lips.

'Quick, she's comin' to.' Seth rolled his blanket and, lifting the woman's head, placed it on the ground. 'That should make it a bit more comfortable, how are you feeling, missy?'

'Where am I?' The woman looked around, saw Seth and Jacob and tried to sit up.

'Now you jus' relax ma'am, get yer bearings and yer strength back,' Jacob went to get the coffee pot, remembered they had no coffee and swore.

'Can't even offer you a coffee, ma'am,

my damned pardner here spilled the last of it.

'That's OK, I'm feeling much better now.' The woman smiled and both men went weak at the knees.

'Glad to hear it, ma'am,' Seth said.

'Samantha,' she said.

'Samantha, nice to meet yer. My name's Seth, this here's my pardner, Jacob.'

'Nice to meet you both. Where exactly am I?' Samantha sat up and felt her head. The wound was only superficial, just a scratch really, which had bled more than it needed to.

'Well, Samantha . . . ' Seth started.

'Sam. Call me Sam, everyone does.'

'OK. Well, Sam, at the moment, you're about sixty miles from Dry Gulch, our hometown,' Seth said.

'What in tarnation are yer doing out here, anyhow. More to the point, how in the hell — sorry ma'am — how on earth did you get out here?' Jacob asked.

'I flew out. I'm learning to fly, and kinda got carried away.'

'Now if that don' beat all. I think that bump on the head was worse than we thought,' Seth laughed.

'How do yer mean 'fly', ma'am?' Jacob asked.

'In the aeroplane,' Sam answered.

'Aerio-plane.' Seth laughed again. 'What in the hell — sorry ma'am — what's an 'aerio-plane'?'

'It's aeroplane, a flying machine. That's what you found me by. I remember trying to start the engine, and then nothing,' Sam said.

'An' you're gonna tell me that runs on steam, right?' Seth asked.

'Good grief no,' Sam answered. 'It's a gasoline engine.'

'Gasoline? I heared o' kerosene, but what's 'gasoline'?' Jacob asked.

'It's similar. I don't really understand just exactly what it is. All I know is it makes the engine run, which makes the aeroplane fly,' Sam said.

'Well I'll be a son of a wh . . . !' Seth stopped himself just in time.

'You mean we got machines now that

can fly?' Jacob asked.

'Sure. Have done for about six or seven years to my knowledge,' Sam said. 'It makes getting about this great country of ours so much easier and quicker.'

'Yeah, so much easier you crashed and damned near killed yerself,' Seth replied.

'Yes. I don't know what happened. Everything was going smoothly, when the engine suddenly lost power. I tried to glide, to get it started, but it wouldn't. Then I just looked for somewhere flattish to land,' Sam said.

'And damn near finished up in the woods there,' Jacob said, but his head was spinning. Flying machines. Great God in heaven, what next? He'd seen the steam engines on the railroad. He'd heard about the automobiles. But flying machines? Hell, he hadn't heard of them.

'Why don' we jus' go and take us a look see at this here machine o' yours,' he said.

'If you're feeling up to it, o' course,' Seth added.

'Yes, I feel just fine, honest.' With that

46

Sam got to her feet, swayed slightly, but was otherwise OK.

'You sure you're up to it, ma'am, you don' look too easy on your feet to me,' Seth said.

'Yes, really. Which way is the plane?' Sam asked.

'Follow me, Sam, it jus' the other side o' these here trees.' Jacob led the way and Sam and Seth followed.

They hadn't gone more than a few yards when Jacob was aware of something moving to his left.

He stopped, raised his left hand to halt the others, and listened.

'What the hell — sorry ma'am — what in the dickens you doing,' asked Seth.

'Thought I heared something.'

'There ain't nothin' there to hear. I didn' hear nothing,' and with that he started moving forward again.

'No, wait. There it is again.' Close by, Jacob heard a twig or branch crack, as if someone had just stood on it. Instinctively, he pulled his gun from its holster, and cocked the hammer. At the same

47

time, Seth slowly drew his Colt, but this time he didn't drop it. Neither did he cock it.

'I can't hear a thing,' Sam whispered. 'What did you hear?'

'I don' rightly know, ma'am. But there sure is something out there,' Jacob whispered back.

'Don' you take no notice, missy, the ol' coot's as deaf as a doorpost.' But Seth still held his un-cocked Colt tightly.

They all stood still, crouching slightly. Silence. They all strained their ears, but there was nothing to hear.

'Guess I was mistaken,' Jacob said, reholstering his weapon.

'You ol' fool. Let's git to this here aeroplane, I gotta see this.' Seth stomped off through the undergrowth, Sam followed, but Jacob was still uneasy. He'd spent too much of his life out in the open not to trust his instincts. He knew someone, or something, was out there watching. Eventually, he too, followed the other two through the undergrowth.

The aeroplane was clearer now. In the

distance, the sun was just below the horizon, but the warm red rays now pierced the early morning sky, painting out the stars one by one.

Jacob was right in his first assessment of the contraption. Cloth and string. That's what it seemed to be made of. Flimsy, light, and to him it looked lethal.

'I wouldn't get in that thing for all the steak in California!' Seth said, as he walked round the plane. He kicked gently at the broken wheel and it fell to the ground. 'Sorry, ma'am, I didn't mean to damage it or nothin'.'

'I think it's damaged enough already,' Sam said eyeing the machinery.

'How in tarnation does it fly?' Jacob asked.

'With a propeller,' Sam replied. 'This thing at the front here.' She pointed to the wooden propeller, which, miraculously, hadn't been damaged in the crash landing. She then looked over the wings and fuselage and tail wings, to see what damage had been caused. But apart from a few holes in the flimsy material, the superstructure looked in one piece.

It was the undercarriage that caused her concern. From the metal struts that stuck out under the body of the plane was an axle with a wheel at either end, except now one of the struts was bent and the wheel was off.

She knelt down to inspect the damage.

'Looks like there ain't much wrong with it,' Jacob said.

'An' how in the h—, how do you know that. You ain't never seen one o' these here aerio-planes before,' Seth said. 'Think you know everything, don't yer.'

'He's right,' Sam said. 'It looks to be the undercarriage that's taken the brunt. Of course, I don't know why the engine stopped, though.'

'Reckon we can fix up that wheel thing, there,' Jacob said. 'T'ain't too much different from fixin' a wagon wheel, just a bit smaller is all.'

'Yeah, you gonna fix the gasoline engine, too? Mister know-it-all.' Seth picked up the wheel and gave it a good once over.

'Wheel's not broke, anyhow,' he added.

'I'd like to have a look at this here engine, ma'am, if'n you don't have any objections.' Jacob looked at Samantha. He looked like a kid who'd just been given his first pistol. Excitement filled his old face.

'No, of course not. I know roughly how it works. But only very roughly.' With that Sam went to the front of the machine, released two flaps and lifted up the cowling.

Jacob emitted a whistle. 'That sure looks like a complicated piece o' hardware, there, ma'am. Don't reckon I'd know where to start with a thing like that.'

'You could try some hay,' Seth said, 'seems to work on the horses, right enough.'

'That weren't even funny,' Jacob said. Samantha laughed.

She was beginning to like the two old codgers. She was thankful it had been them that had found her. She'd heard many stories of people being bush-whacked, or worse still, to her, raped or

51

murdered out on the plains.

She'd been warned when she wanted to learn to fly about getting lost, or flying over the wild country, of what could happen if anything went wrong. But she'd laughed.

Samantha had come out West from Boston. She'd grown up in her banker father's house, her mother had died in childbirth. She was the youngest of three, the elder two being boys. So, not unnaturally, she grew up to be a tomboy. Her father had hired a succession of governesses, trying to turn his beloved daughter into a young lady, but to no avail. Samantha Gibbons was to be what she was to be.

Eventually, her father had to accept her for what she was. He did so lovingly.

Samantha had always been restless, high-spirited, a daredevil. Boston was a 'nice' place, and Samantha didn't like it. Not one bit.

When the West began to open up, she begged her father to let her go. Adamantly, he refused. There had been too many stories in the Boston newspapers about the killings, the Indians, the Mexicans, gunslingers, not to mention the natural hazards. No, the West was not hospitable enough for his daughter.

However, when she became of age, there was no holding her back.

Fate struck a hand. There in the *Boston Journal* was an advertisement feature. The flying machine was coming of age.

The year was 1903. The Wright Brothers had first flown an aeroplane the previous December down in Kitty Hawk and the whole country was excited.

Samantha was, of course, immediately sold on the idea of flying.

There were arguments, her brothers, both now bankers, couldn't understand why she didn't settle down, get married and produce babies, like all the other women. *Flying!* Preposterous, especially for a woman.

That lit the fuse. Samantha's inheritance was more than enough to purchase both the aeroplane and the means to transport it West and learn to fly it. And that's exactly what she did and why she was where she was.

Samantha began to explain to both Seth and Jacob the little she knew about the aeroplane's engine. Seth, for his part, was not in the slightest bit interested. You can't teach an old dog new tricks. Surprisingly, Jacob was all ears. Quickly, he began to grasp the rudimentary facts of the engine. He seemed to be a natural.

Of course, he had always been handy with his hands, with a partner like Seth, he had to be. Now he was excited — he understood.

'Looks to me like the fuel line's come adrift. You were damn lucky the thing didn't explode,' Jacob said as he set to work reconnecting the fuel line.

'Fuel line? Where in the hell an' all did yer learn that one?' Seth said.

'Easy, fool. I bin listenin' to the young lady here.'

'So have I an' I never heared no 'fuel line' being mentioned.' Seth was obviously agitated, he hadn't been listening.

'Well, you heared it now, ain't yer!'

Jacob had connected the fuel line, stood back, wiped his hand on the back of his jeans and said: 'Reckon you can try it agin, now, ma'am.'

'Please, call me Sam. You make me sound like an old spinster,' Samantha laughed as she turned on the ignition and went to the front of the plane.

'Well, here goes.' With that she placed both hands on the wooden propeller, and with all her strength, which wasn't all that much, she gave the propeller a pull.

Nothing happened.

She tried again, the result was the same.

'Here, ma'am — er Sam — let me have a go of that thing,' Seth stepped forward.

'Oh, thanks. Be careful to step back though, this thing can chop your arms off,' Sam warned him.

'Sure thing, Sam.' Seth placed his gnarled hands on the propeller and gave it a mighty pull. The engine almost caught, but not quite. Seth had jumped back so quickly that, hitting a small rock, he fell over backwards. Both Sam and Jacob fell about laughing.

'All right, all right. It ain't that funny,' Seth said as he picked himself up, dusted himself off, and grabbed hold of the propeller again.

This time, the engine spluttered, coughed, then burst into life.

'Oh, Seth, Jacob, that's wonderful! You did it, you did it.' Sam was beside herself with glee.

'T'wern't nothin', Sam.' Seth was slightly embarrassed.

'Now all we got to do, is fix this here wheel thing, so's you can get back in the air again,' Jacob said.

The noise from the engine was both deafening and alien to the prairie. Both the Indian party and the four cowboys almost jumped out of their skins when the engine exploded into life.

The Indians were sure convinced that Manitou was with them. This gave them the courage and strength to tackle anything. The four young cowboys were just scared witless. All that is except Lewis; he was as excited as ever.

'Come on, let's go see what that is,' he said.

'Are you outta yer mind! We don' know what in the hell that is. Sounds like a Gatlin' gun to me,' James said. 'Let's just take it easy. We already had more'n our fair share of bad luck.'

'We can't jus' not do nothin',' Lewis said.

'We ain't gonna do jus' nothin'. We're gonna plan somethin'. We're gonna circle round, carefully, and take a look-see at whatever that din is. Now, Hank, Brad, you go to the left, Lewis, you come with me.' With that the four got their guns out and moved off.

★ ★ ★

The Indian party worked in silence. Sign language was the order of the day. Of the three groups of people in the prairie, they were the only ones who knew about the other two. Silently, they edged forward towards the sound of Manitou. At the edge of the copse they stopped. They stared.

What they saw was not Manitou. They didn't know what it was. Their courage started to desert them.

At the same time the four men had circled from the other side. They too stopped and stared.

Seth was the first to be aware that they were not on their own. Slowly he drew his gun. Jacob noticed, and, without a word, he too drew his weapon. Sam was oblivious.

Seth and Jacob instinctively moved back-to-back, handguns cocked. They were surrounded. Indians to the left and right, white men in front and behind.

'Seems like we got a mess o' company, Jacob.'

'Seems that way, Seth.'

With that, Sam shrieked, 'Indians, there's Indians in the trees!'

6

The immediate reaction of three of the Indians was to run. They ran scared out of their minds, back to their ponies and away. The other three stood still, wanting to run, but their pride wouldn't let them.

Seth and Jacob knew they were well outnumbered, a movement behind them caused Jacob to turn.

'What in the hell of damnation is that?' It was James who spoke first. Although his handgun was out, it was hanging by his side.

'We don' want no trouble here, mister,' Seth said.

'We don't aim to cause none.' James stepped forward, holstering his gun. Lewis followed.

Jacob stood his ground. 'That's far enough, mister, now jus' drop yer guns.'

James motioned to Brad and Hank. They both dropped their guns, followed by James and Lewis. Seth and Jacob kept theirs out, but more for the three braves who were still staring.

The four white men reached the aeroplane and stood marvelling. Seth moved away from Jacob, motioning to the Indians to come forward.

The three Indians also dropped their weapons and came forward to stand by the aeroplane.

An impasse had been reached. Seth and Jacob didn't quite know what to do. Their adversaries, if that's what they were, had all dropped their weapons and, with the exception of James, who couldn't take his eyes off Samantha, the rest of the men were just looking at the aeroplane.

Seth turned to Jacob, 'Well what in the hell do we do now?'

'I guess we could start off with introductions,' Jacob replied.

'How do you do, my name's Samantha, but everyone calls me Sam.' Sam held her hand out to James.

Immediately he whisked off his dust-laden hat, wiped his hand on the back of his breeches and said, 'Mighty pleased to meet you, ma'am. My name's James, this here is Hank, Lewis and Brad.'

Each in turn removed their hats and said 'howdy ma'am' in embarrassed tones.

Sam then took a deep breath and approached the three Indians. It was the first time she had even seen an Indian, let alone met one. She held her hand out and introduced herself. Immediately she was taken aback.

'Pleased to meet you, Sam. My name is Running Tree, these are my brothers, Wolf Wind and Moonface.'

'You speak perfect English!' Sam couldn't hide her surprise.

'We were taught it as children back on the reservation,' Running Tree replied.

'Well, I'm Seth and this here's Jacob.'

Muttered hullos went on, then silence.

'Excuse me for askin', ma'am. But what in all that's holy is this contraption?' James enquired.

The lengthy explanations were gone over again for the benefit of the new-comers.

'Trouble is,' said Seth, 'none of us know enough about this here thing to get it up again.'

It was decided that the aeroplane be pulled from its resting place and pushed out on to the prairie. Seth and Jacob got to work on the bent undercarriage, while Lewis and his gang set about the wheel. The three Indians stood and watched in silence.

'Wouldn't it be wonderful if we could get it flying again,' Sam said, 'I could take each of you up in turn so you'd know what it was like.'

Jacob was the first to react. 'That sure would be something, Sam. I figure that's one thing I'd sure like to do before I die.'

'That may be the last you do before you die,' Seth muttered.

Eventually, they were ready. Sam climbed into the rear cockpit and turned on the ignition. Jacob stood by the propeller, waiting her instructions. 'Right, Jacob, give it your best,' Sam said.

Jacob spat on his hands, rubbed them together, and placed them on the topmost propeller. 'One, two, three.' And with that he gave the propeller a mighty pull.

Nothing.

'Goddamnit,' he muttered under his breath.

'OK, try again, now,' Sam shouted.

'Here, let me give you a hand,' James stepped forward, took his range-coat off, and placed his hands next to Jacob's.

'Get ready to step back if it fires,' warned Sam.

'OK, now. One, two, three,' Jacob said and this time, the mighty tug had the engine coughing and spluttering before it died out.

'Next time should do it,' Sam shouted excitedly.

'Next time, I think the ol' coot's gonna have a seizure,' Seth remarked laconically.

This time, the engine coughed, spluttered, and then sprang into life. From all around, the din of the engine had the wildlife running scared,

Jacob and James had leapt backwards as the propeller started to spin. Jacob couldn't take his eyes off it, he'd never seen anything move so fast. 'Goddamn, if'n the thing spins so quick, you can't even see it!'

Seth moved beside his companion and helped him to his feet. 'You dang ol' fool, could'a broken somethin', fallin' down like that.

'Stop your goddamn motherin', will you?' Jacob flustered, wiping the trail dust off his clothes.

James picked himself up, put his coat back on, and also stood watching the propeller. It was mesmeric.

Sam jumped from the aeroplane and thanked the two men. 'Now to see if the undercarriage will hold up to a take-off and landing.' With that she crossed her fingers, placed the leather helmet and goggles on her head, and clambered, quite unladylike, back aboard the aeroplane.

Jacob motioned to the assembled company to turn the aeroplane round, and point it at the relatively flat prairie.

'How d'you know which way the damn

thing's to go?' Seth asked.

'Well if'n you'd been payin' attention earlier, you'd know, so quit your moanin' and push,' Jacob replied.

'Well, ex-cu-se me!' Seth murmured.

The aeroplane, with nine men pushing, was easily moved. The only problem was that none of the men could see much. The propeller had whipped up a regular sandstorm, as well as sending at least two hats back into the copse.

'Right,' Sam shouted, 'this should do it. Wish me luck.'

With that, the engine pitch increased and the aeroplane began to bump its way forward over the sand and patchy grass. The men stood and watched, not really knowing what to expect. The aeroplane's speed increased, and then, after one or two bumps and hops, it was airborne.

There were great whoops of delight as the aeroplane hit the skies.

'Well I'll be a . . . ' Seth began.

'That sure is a purty sight,' Jacob said.

'That's the weirdest thing I ever did see,' joined in James.

Lewis was dumbstruck.

The three Indians did a little war dance.

Hank and Brad stood with their mouths open.

From the aeroplane, Sam waved, and, spontaneously, all the men waved and jumped and yelled 'ya-hoo'.

* * *

Unbeknown to the small group, a gang of saddle-bums had also seen the aeroplane take-off. And, far from being excited or delighted, all they could see were dollar signs flashing in front of their eyes.

Sam swept across the prairie, banked to the left, then the right, pulled the joystick up until the ground disappeared, and then forward so that all she could see was the ground rushing up to meet her. The little aeroplane did exactly as she told it. No damage had been done to the control wires. Sam began to relax and enjoy the flight.

Now came the crunch, metaphorically

speaking, she thought to herself. If Seth and Jacob had done a good job on the undercarriage, there shouldn't be any problems. On the other hand . . . Well, she didn't really want to think of the other hand.

Reducing speed and angling a descent pattern, Sam eased the aeroplane lower and lower. She hadn't done that many landings, but was aware of not going too slow; she'd had plenty of crash-landings caused by stalling. She kept her eyes firmly on the horizon, and began to gauge how low she was, listening to the engine to judge her speed. *Keep the nose up. Whatever you do, keep the nose up.*

Slowly, the aeroplane sank lower and lower. On the ground, the men stood watching. They knew there was nothing they could do, and were completely unaware of the thoughts going through Sam's mind. All, that is, except Jacob. He had a sneaky feeling that this was some sort of a test, both for Sam and the machine. Although he had no doubts as to his own workmanship, this was something else.

For what seemed like hours, the small band watched as the aeroplane got closer and closer to the ground. They could see that flying was about as smooth as riding a horse as the aeroplane bumped along in the air, sometimes rising by ten or so feet, then plummeting back down again. Jacob wasn't sure if the controls weren't working as they should, or if Sam's expertise was lacking a little.

They held their collective breaths as the plane first bumped on to the ground, jumped up a few feet, bumped again and then gradually slowed to a walking pace not more than a hundred yards from where they stood. As the soon as the engine was cut, the 'ya-hoos' began again and nine very excited men ran towards the motionless machine.

Sam jumped from the cockpit, pulled off the hat and goggles. Her smile was a mile wide. 'We did it, we did it!' she screamed.

'We sure as hell did!' shouted Jacob, and gave her a bear hug that very nearly pulled all the air out of her lungs. 'That was the best thing I ever did see.'

'Thanks to you, thanks to you all!' Sam said with glee.

Lewis was practically beside himself, he was so excited.

Even Seth, careful not to show too much pleasure, managed a wry grin. 'Yeah, well, 't'wern't nothin' really,' he managed to say, and nonchalantly leant one hand on the engine cowling. 'Goddamn, blast-it-to-hell-an'-back,' he shouted and jumped up and down, waving his slightly burnt hand in the air and blowing on it.

'Seth, are you all right?' Sam asked.

'Excuse me, ma'am, for cussing an' all, I didn't realise that engine thing got so hell-fire hot,' Seth said, calming down slightly.

'Here, wrap this scarf round your hand,' Sam offered.

'No need young missy, more surprised than hurt,' Seth replied.

'How many people can fit into this here aeroplane, Sam?' asked Lewis.

'Well, as you can see, there are two cockpits, the front one is purely for the ride, the one at the rear has all the controls in it. Why? Would you like to go up with me, Lewis?' Sam asked, knowing full well what the answer would be.

'Oh, no, ma'am, I was jus' curious, is all.' Immediately, Lewis changed his mind. If a woman could fly, then so could he! 'Yes. I'd give anything to go up in it.' Lewis said.

'Well, let's get this plane turned around and off we'll go,' Sam said.

Once more they turned the plane around to face the smooth prairie, Sam pulled on her hat and goggles, and Lewis clambered into the front cockpit.

No one saw the masked men sneak up behind them, guns already drawn. 'Well, now, what do we have ourselves here?' one of the men said. 'I suggest you all just put your hands in the air and step away from that there machine.'

7

Seth's immediate reaction was to try and draw his gun, but Jacob quickly thwarted that. He'd seen the way Seth could draw, and he didn't fancy his chances. Slowly, everyone raised their hands.

'Well now, what a nice little party we have ourselves here,' their leader said. 'Guess we'll jus' take a look around here. Joe, you keep these nice folks covered, and take their weapons.'

The tall man walked towards Seth and Jacob, a Navy Colt in each hand, an unlit cheroot between his lips. His face was scarred, he obviously hadn't shaved for a week, and the closer he got, the more apparent it became he hadn't washed none to recently either.

'We ain't got nothin' here that would interest you folks,' Jacob offered.

'Now you jus' keep your fat mouth closed, ol' man, else I'll close it for you.' The reply made Jacob shiver. There was

71

death in this man's eyes. Jacob knew he'd shoot any or all of them given the slightest excuse, and there wouldn't be too much remorse shown afterwards.

'Who are you, and what do you want?' demanded Sam.

'Well, now. Sassy li'l miss, ain't we.' The tall man removed his hat, not out of any respect for a lady, but so he could get a better view.

'Now forgive mah mahnners,' he said using a false Southern drawl, and then he made an exaggerated bow. 'Mah name's Burt, ma'am, this here's Joe. The rest of 'em prob'ly have names, but I don't rightly recall any of 'em at the moment.' Burt held a mocking sneer on his face as he looked at Sam from her hair to her face, to her chest, to her waist, and slowly down to her feet, before focusing back on her face again. The look he gave her left nothing to the imagination.

'An' you are?' Burt asked.

'Not that it's any of your business, but my name's Samantha, and these people are . . .'

'I ain't a whole lot in'erested in these folks, ma'am, but I'm sure as hell in'erested in you,' Burt sidled up to Sam and walked around her, eyeing her up all the time. It reminded Seth of eyeing up a prize steer.

'Purty nice, pur-ty nice, ma'am,' Burt said at last.

'What about the fancy buggy here, Burt?' It was the first time that Joe had opened his mouth.

'Shut the hell up an' do as you're told. If'n there's any questions to askin', *I'll* do the askin'. Got it?' Burt shouted across.

'Sure, boss, anythin' you say, just wonderin' was all,' Joe whined.

'Now, where was we, missy?' Burt said to Sam.

'We weren't anywhere,' she replied.

'Oh, but we're gonna be, oh yes siree, we gonna be.' His laugh chilled Sam to the bone.

'Now what in the hell an' all is this here fancy buggy doin' out in the middle of nowhere?' Burt asked.

'It ain't no buggy,' Seth spoke out, 'It's

a aereoplane.'

'Say what?' Burt asked.

'An aeroplane,' Jacob offered, 'a flying machine, is all.'

'You take me for a fool, ol' man?' Burt was threatening again.

'No, don't figure you to be no fool, but that's what it is, right enough,' Jacob answered.

Before anyone could react, Burt brought one of the Navy Colt's down on the side of Jacob's head, sending him sprawling into the sand, where he didn't move. Seth made to move, but Burt cocked the pistol and looked at him. 'Go on, ol' timer, give it your best shot.'

'No, Seth,' Sam said. 'I'll take care of him.'

Sam knelt by Jacob's side, the blood covering his face made her stomach turn, this sort of thing never happened in Boston. She tore off a strip of her skirt and dabbed at Jacob's head. The wound was not deep, but the blood was steady. Tearing off another strip, this time from her petticoat, she fashioned a bandage and tied it to Jacob's head. Quickly, a crimson patch appeared, but the blood had stopped oozing down his face.

'There was no need for that,' she spat.

'I don' need no need, ma'am, I jus' do it.' With that Burt started to laugh again, a maniacal laugh. Joe joined in, until Burt looked in his direction.

'Sorry, boss,' he said.

In the instant Burt looked round, Moonface leapt towards him, knife in hand. The move was quick, but not quick enough. With nonchalant ease, Burt levelled on the Colts and fired. Moonface was struck in the chest in mid-flight. He crashed to ground and groaned. The other two Indians stepped towards their wounded brother, until Burt halted them in their tracks.

'Now where do you two redskins think you're goin'?' Burt said.

He laughed again, pointed one of the pistols at the wounded Indian and fired, almost point blank straight between the eyes.

Moonface's head exploded.

Sam fainted. Jacob came to as the bullet struck Moonface. He felt his own head, then noticed that he was covered in blood and gore. At first he thought it was his own brains he was staring at, relief that it wasn't was tempered by wondering who the hell had been shot.

'Now, unless anyone else has any ideas on bein' a hero . . . ' Burt left the sentence unfinished. It was clear now to the rest of the party that this man would kill them all.

Joe left his position and went to the dead Indian's side, removed the knife from his death grip and turned to Burt. 'Can I have it, please, huh, Burt? Can I, can I?'

Burt looked down at Joe. There was a distinct look of hatred for the man on his face. 'What in the hell d'you want that for, you crazy sonofawhore?' He fired two more shots into the dead body of Moonface, narrowly missing Joe, who flung himself backwards, hitting Seth and bringing him to the ground.

'Don't shoot me, boss,' Joe screamed.

'You can 'ave it. Honest, I don' wan' it, I don' wan' it.'

Joe collapsed on the ground, holding his head in his hands and crying 'I don' wan' it, I don' wan' it.' Then Burt stepped up and kicked him hard in the ribs.

'Get the hell up, you snivellin' worm.' Burt kicked him again.

Joe jumped to his feet, stopped whinging, and backed off to the far side of the group.

The other members of the gang, which, as far as Seth could make out, numbered seven in total, had neither moved, nor said a word. He glanced at Jacob, who, unarmed, could think of nothing to convey to Seth.

Burt settled his stone-like eyes on Sam again. 'Quite a little nurse, ain't we, see what you can do for the Indian, here.' Again he laughed. He was obviously enjoying himself immensely.

Sam was still nauseous, and had not yet regained her feet. 'You bastard,' she muttered.

Burt, as luck would have it, did not hear what she said.

'So, this here's a flying machine, huh. Don' seem to be doin' much flying, does it.' With that he reached out with his left foot and tentatively kicked one of the plane's wheels. He took a quick step back.

Jacob observed this and knew straight away that this 'onery killer was afraid of the machine. He might be able to use that to his advantage.

'What makes it fly then?' Burt asked.

'Well, kicking it doesn't,' Sam replied.

Burt whipped round, a demonic look in his eyes, he may not have had much intelligence, but he knew sarcasm when he heard it. And sarcasm riled him. Especially in front of his men, even though they had less sense than he did.

'You got a mouth on you, missy', he said threateningly. 'You wanna watch that.'

Sam believed him.

'Now I'll ask again. What makes it fly?'

'I do,' Sam said.

'Yeah, sure. I tol' you to watch your mouth,' Burt said.

'No, I mean it, I fly the aeroplane. I'm the pilot.' Sam raised herself to her feet, with the aid of Jacob's arm. 'Would you like me to show you?'

'Now you mus' think I got no brains at all. I let you near that thing, an' off you go right? Well, missy, I'll tell you this. Sure, you show me how this thing works, an' if'n you don' come back here, all these nice folks, includin' the boy . . .' But he was cut short by Lewis.

'I ain't no boy!'

Surprisingly, Burt ignored him altogether. 'As I said, including the boy, will be kilt, one by one every five minutes 'til there ain't nothing here but blood and gore for the buzzards to feed on. Tell you what, I'll start with the knee-caps and work my way up. What'ya think, huh?' Burt laughed again.

'I'll come back, you have my word on it,' Sam said.

'OK, then. Joe, you an' the boys tie these folks up so's we can watch without havin' to worry about 'em.'

Joe went to the horses and he, along with two of the other men, began tying up their prisoners.

'Nice and tight now, we don't want any more heroes here, now do we,' Burt said.

Sam put the flying helmet and goggles on and stepped up into the cockpit. She turned on the ignition and waited.

'What the hell you waitin' fer?' Burt shouted.

'I need someone to turn the propeller. That thing,' she pointed to the front of the aeroplane. 'If you could pull it round, it'll start the engine, then I can fly it.'

'You take me for a fool, I tol' you no more heroes!' Burt levelled his gun.

'It's true,' Jacob said. 'You have to turn the propeller, if'n you untie these 'ere ropes, I'll do it.'

'No. You jus' stay where you are ol' man. Joe, you pull the propeller.'

Joe's eyes widened in fear. 'I ain't never done none of that afore. Why me? Why not one of them?' He pointed to the other men.

'OK, you chickenshit, yellow-bellied skunk. You,' he shouted at the nearest man, 'start the propeller.'

The short, pot-bellied man holstered his gun and, without a word, walked to the front of the aeroplane.

'OK,' said Sam, 'Pull it clockwise from the top, but pull hard.'

The man stepped forward, placed both hands on the wooden propeller and tugged down as hard as he could. His size belied his strength, which, coupled with the fact the engine was still warm, was enough to fire the engine first time. Unfortunately for Pot-belly, no one had told him to stand away from the propeller. Just as the engine burst into life, the propeller caught Pot-belly on his left shoulder, cutting off both shoulder and arm in one fell swoop. This pulled Pot-belly forward, and before he could even utter a scream, the blades of the propeller caught his neck and severed his head clean off his remaining shoulder.

Sam was unaware of this until the hot

red spray of blood hit her full in the face. She screamed, and, standing up, she went to climb out of the aeroplane.

'You stay put, right where you are,' Burt said. 'Now get that thing up in the air, or I start shootin'.'

Sam sat down again and started to taxi off, the engine picked up speed and, hardly believing his eyes, Burt watched in amazement as the wheels left the ground and the whole contraption was in the air.

Sam flew the aeroplane round in a large circle and then landed again, coming to rest more or less in the place she had started, but facing the other way.

Burt moved out of the way of the propellers, not sure what it was that was spinning so fast at the front of the machine, but it sure had made a mess of Pot-belly.

Sam cut the engine and stepped out of the cockpit. Removing her helmet and goggles, she went to Jacob's side without saying a word.

'Well I'll be doggoned, if that ain't the weirdest thing I ever did see,' Burt said.

'Seems to me that could be a mighty useful machine you got there, in the right hands. Wouldn't get no posse following that, now, would we?'

Burt walked slowly around the aeroplane, touching it gingerly. He motioned to his gang to bring the wagon up to the plane.

'Seein' as how I ain't learned how to fly this thing yet, missy, reckon we'll just load it on the wagon here and take off. 'Course, that means you'll have to come with us, but I 'spect you ain't gonna put up no fight now, are you?' Burt leaned close to Sam. The stench of both him, and his breath, almost made her gag.

'I'll come gladly, but on one condition,' she said, trying to keep her voice calm.

'You ain't got no conditions, lady, you're comin' and that's all there is to it,' Burt shouted, rage showing in his eyes.

'If you want me to fly that thing, and then teach you to fly it, I have one condition,' she repeated.

'Well come on then, what's your 'condition'?' Burt said.

Sam took a deep breath. 'My condition is that you don't kill any more people here. We ride out of here and you leave them all alone.'

Burt laughed. He laughed a long time. But his laughter merely served as thinking time for him. He could agree to her terms, and then send back two or three men to kill the rest of the party at night, when out of earshot. Or he could just shoot them all, force Sam to come with them, and then persuade her by fair means, but preferably by foul means, to teach him to fly.

'OK. Deal.' he raised his hand as if to shake, then spat on it, and offered it again.

Gingerly, Sam shook hands as the rest of the gang manhandled the aeroplane on to the flatbed of the wagon, and roped it down securely. Burt checked the ropes on the prisoners.

Turning to Sam he said, 'Jus' so's we both know what the score is, lady, I'll jus' give you a little some-thin' to think about as we travel on.' With that he drew one of his pistols, walked around the little group, and without seeming to care who it was, aimed the pistol at James's arm and fired.

The bullet hit James in the lower arm, just below the elbow. One inch higher and the arm would have been shot off. The bullet went clean through, missing bones and, fortunately for James, the artery.

Sam screamed, 'You promised me, no more killing.'

'I ain't killed him, jus' wounded a little, is all,' Burt grinned.

James, teeth gritted, had not uttered a sound, but the pain was almost unbearable. There was very little blood, which was a good sign, but the pain was excruciating.

Burt climbed aboard his horse and, turning said, 'Now you boys take care, an' don't git any fancy ideas on followin'. I'll kill her as easy as pie if'n I have to. Now you think on that.' Nodding to his men, Burt instructed them to help them get some sleep. Three men dismounted and, with their pistols out, they struck each man in turn across the back of the head.

With that, the party rode off without even looking back.

Sam, however, never looked to the front. She sat mutely on the wagon seat, silent tears flowed down her cheeks. Not knowing whether they were alive or dead.

8

One by one, the men came to, with blinding headaches. But they still noticed the smell. The dead bodies were already beginning to attract insects. From nowhere they came out in their hundreds. Ants and beetles to begin with, but soon the smell of decay would bring the buzzards.

The buzzards would gather, and in their turn they would signal all the other animals on the prairie, albeit unwittingly. Seth and Jacob knew what danger they were in. Not just because they were tied hand and foot in the middle of nowhere, with darkness approaching with no water, no horses and no food, but because if they didn't manage to get free soon, they could get eaten alive by the insects or, maybe worse, the odd mountain lion or two.

'Anybody got any bright ideas?' Jacob asked.

'Seems like my arm's a little dead,' James said. 'Can't feel too much of my hand.'

'At least the bleeding weren't too bad,' Seth offered.

Lewis managed to get himself in a sitting position. Being the youngest, he felt that he stood the best chance of getting himself free. 'If I can just get some movement, I might be able to loosen these ropes enough to get them off.'

'Goddamn, boy, if'n any of us could get some movement we'd all be able to get the ropes off.' Seth had little time for the young.

Wolf Wind and Running Tree also managed to get themselves in an upright position. Unbeknown to the others, Wolf Wind kept a knife in his boot. Running Tree turned sideways on and took the knife in both hands, then, turning, began to cut at the ropes that bound Wolf Wind's hands.

In seconds, Wolf Wind's hands were free. He quickly untied the ropes at his feet, released Running Tree and both men stood.

'Well, come on, cut the rest of us free,' Lewis shouted.

'We go now, to avenge the death of our brother,' Running Tree said matter-of-factly.

'Seems like we got ourselves some avenging, too,' Jacob said. 'Might be a good idea, seeing as how we ain't got no weapons, or horses, to team up and catch them *hombres* before they get too far away. What d'you say?'

Both Indians looked toward each other, a silent agreement was formed. Without saying a word, Running Tree cut the ropes off each man.

'We join together, but the man Burt is ours, agreed?' Running Tree said.

'Agreed,' Jacob replied.

'Any idea how long we been out?' Jacob asked as he helped James to his feet, stripped off his jacket and shirt and inspected the wound in James's arm.

'Ain't too bad, boy. We'll bandage it up some, but we'll have to clean that wound soon, or infection will get in there.' Jacob busied himself ripping James's shirt to fashion a bandage.

'Let's get a look at your head, Jacob. Don't want you goin' a looney on us.' Seth wiped at Jacob's head with another part of James's shirt.

'Take more'n that to rattle my brains, Seth,' Jacob said.

'Who said anythin' 'bout brains. I never did think you had none too many o' them.' Seth made a wry grin as he inspected the wound.

'Quit your fussin'. Ain't nothin' wrong up there, you damned ol' fool'. Jacob brushed Seth's hands away from his head and finished the bandage on James's arm. 'That should hold it for a while. I'll turn the rest of your shirt into a sling, that'll ease the pain a bit. Jus' try and keep it as still as you can,' Jacob said, tying the shirt tail behind James's head and gently lifting his injured arm into the makeshift sling.

Both Indians were scouring the copse. They were looking for their own ponies, which they'd left on the far side. Both were hoping that they were still there, along with the tomahawks they'd left tied around the ponies' necks.

They found their mounts exactly where they'd left them, calmly eating at the sparse grass that managed to force its way out of the parched earth. Silently, they mounted their steeds and headed back to the others.

In the meantime, Seth, Jacob, Lewis, Hank and Brad were searching through the undergrowth, looking for any of the weapons they'd been forced to drop on their first meeting.

Burt may have been the leader of the gang, but he wasn't exactly endowed with much brainpower. Although he'd taken Seth's and Jacob's side-arms, he didn't think anything strange about the other four being unarmed.

Lewis was the first to find a gun, 'Got one, it's yours, James.' He ran to James's side and handed him the weapon.

'Thanks, Lewis, now see if you can find the rest,' James holstered his weapon, and slowly got to his feet.

One by one, the other three weapons were found. The Indians arrived back at the campsite and offered Jacob and James their mounts. James accepted gratefully, but Jacob was man enough, if not entirely well enough, to at first refuse, but eventually, with a bit a prodding from Seth, he mounted the Indian's pony.

'We lead and follow tracks,' Wolf Wind said, and without waiting for any discussion, he started to walk off. It was Running Tree who halted him in his tracks.

'Wait, my brother. Surely you forget.' Running Tree looked towards the crumpled bloody mess that was Moonface.

'Forgive me, my mind is filled with hate, I was thinking only of revenge,' Wolf Wind said quietly.

'It is only natural my brother, but first we must honour our dead brother,' Running Tree said.

Without another word, they began gathering branches, using their knives and tomahawks to cut off bigger branches.

'What in the blazes are you two doin'?' James asked. 'We ain't got no time for a funeral.'

'Our brother must be sent to the Happy Hunting grounds, his soul must be elevated so that the gods may receive his spirit. It is something we must do,' Running Tree said without stopping in his task.

'He's right, James. Mebbe we should bury him, too.' Seth said pointing to the dismembered body of Pot-belly.

'I'd leave him for the buzzards,' Lewis said, but he didn't look towards the body, as he knew he'd be sick all over the place. And that would not do.

'Let's gather some rocks together, an' cover him up,' Seth Said.

So, with the exception of James, who was too injured to help, they set about the task of covering Pot-belly.

Running Tree and Wolf Wind gently raised the body of their dead brother atop the rickety table of branches that they had expertly constructed. They folded his arms across his chest, placed a knife in one hand and a tomahawk in the other, and straightened his legs. They stood back respectfully, silence filled the air, then they began their chant. Holding small, leaved twigs, they gently hit themselves and the funeral platform, never stopping their chant.

Seth and Jacob in particular, actually found the whole scene quite moving, especially when they looked from the solemn-faced Indians treating their dead brother with reverence, and then looked over at Hank and Brad and Lewis, who were tossing rocks on to Pot-belly as if they were shovelling coal.

'Take more care, there,' Jacob said. 'He has a mother somewhere.'

'Yeah, well she ain't got no son no more,' Lewis said. Nevertheless, they all started placing, rather than throwing, the rocks on the body.

Seth and Jacob meandered over to the Indians and removed their hats.

'Jus' thought we'd pay our last respects, too,' Seth muttered.

'We not know the white man has a soul,' Running Tree said.

'Yeah, well, mebbe some of us ain't,' Seth said, 'but your brother there was one of us, and he tried to help.'

'Thank you for your respects,' Wolf Wind said quietly.

'You're welcome,' Seth replied.

'If'n we don't get goin' soon, we ain't never gonna catch 'em.' The impatience in Lewis's voice all too apparent.

'Hold your horses, son,' Jacob said soothingly, 'It'll be night time soon. Ain't no sense in running off half-cocked. They ain't gonna do much travellin' during the darkness, an' neither are we.'

'But we'll never be able to pick up their tracks,' Lewis stated.

'Only human beings cover their tracks,' Running Tree said. 'The white man leaves his mark on nature wherever he goes. We will not lose them.'

★ ★ ★

The camp-fire was still glowing as the spidery fingers of dawn began to creep across the prairie. Seth was awake in seconds. A lifetime of sleeping under the stars had honed his senses to the extent that he felt he could even smell the sun rising.

He ached everywhere. Back, shoulders, hips, legs; if he could move it, it was sore. He knew that Jacob was feeling the years every bit as much as he was. But what could they do? They knew no other life. Sure, they'd slept in beds before, always found them too soft in the past, but now? Seth kinda thought he'd like to give them another go.

Slowly, he raised himself on to one elbow, waited for the pain to subside, then sat up. The sun had almost cleared the mountains to the east, the air had that fresh smell that only dawn can give it.

Rising slowly to his feet, he stretched — at least, he stretched as far as he could — picked his gun up from beneath the rough grass he'd fashioned as a pillow, and holstered it. Then he scratched his balls, yawned and wandered off to take a leak.

Gradually, the camp awoke. Lewis put more kindling on the fire and managed to keep it going. Seth wandered back to the fire and warmed his hands, it would be a couple of hours yet before the sun's rays took the coldness out of the night air.

'Seems like them Indians high-tailed it outta here,' Jacob said.

'I can't believe they'd jus' leave,' Seth said.

'They's only In'ians, what'd you expect!' Lewis said.

'Yeah, an' you know all about 'In'ians', don't you, boy,' Jacob spat.

'Well, I know they're savages. They're heathens. They ain' like us,' Lewis said defensively.

'You ever knowed any, boy?' Seth said.

'I read about 'em plenty,' Lewis said and started to wander off to take a leak.

' 'Read' about 'em. A young whipper-snapper like you. You mean you can read an' all?' Seth said.

'Sure. Taught at school. Wasn' everybody?' Lewis said over his shoulder.

It was as well that Lewis didn't hear Seth's reply.

'They'll be back. You mark my words,' Jacob offered.

'How's the arm, James?' Hank asked.

'Wondering when you'd speak any, boy,' Seth said with a wry grin.

'No point in sayin' anythin' if you ain't got nothin' to say,' Hank replied.

'Sore, but OK, I guess,' James said. 'Leastways, I ain't gonna die, not just yet anyways.'

'We'd better be moving off. Sun's full up now, we should be able to follow that buckboard's tracks without too much of a problem.' Jacob began to kick sand over the fire, just as it was beginning to burn right.

Looking around, both Seth and Jacob decided there wasn't anything of use they could take with them, except, of course, their weapons. Jacob asked for, and received, James's weapon. Seth was upset about that, but as Jacob explained to James, Seth was safer without a gun; he'd learnt that from bitter experience.

Walking, in boots, through sand, is not an easy job. Walking, when you're a cowboy and used to riding everywhere, is a chore. It only took Seth five minutes to start moaning.

'Goddamn-in-hell, if'n these boots ain't made for walkin', my feet are afire already.'

'Well, you'd better get used to it, pard-ner, seems like we're fixing to do a lot a walking before the day's out,' Jacob said good-humouredly.

At the sound of horses, all six men dropped to the floor, guns ready, hardly daring to move. At first they thought Burt had had second thoughts about leaving them all alive, and had either come back personally to have a bit of fun shooting them, or had sent one of his henchman to do the job for him.

There was no need to worry; as Jacob had predicted, it was Running Tree and Wolf Wind returning.

'Was beginning to wonder whether we'd see you two boys again,' Seth said.

'We follow tracks, find their campsite, fire still burning. One man dead, shot in back.' It was Running Tree who described the scene.

'Looks like there was argument, two men, big fight, one now dead. One less for us to worry about.'

'Yeah, but it makes me worry what the fight was about,' James interjected. 'Where there's a woman involved, an' I bet they haven't seen a woman for a while. I hope to God she's OK'

'Seems like you might be a bit soft on her, James,' Jacob said. 'Mighty purty woman, I have to agree with you, there, mighty purty.'

'Full o' spunk, too, flyin' an' all,' Seth said.

'How far ahead would you say they are, Running Tree?' Jacob asked.

'Not more than one half-day, buggy slow moving, we should be near by end of sun.'

'Not if'n we're walking all day,' Seth

said. 'Seems like they can travel faster than we can.'

'Well, if'n you're in agreement,' Jacob said to Running Tree and Wolf Wind, 'I suggest that we take turns on them there ponies. James and Seth take first ride, at least that'll shut him up for a while.'

'We will scout ahead, mark the track and watch out in case of ambush,' Wolf Wind said.

With that, both men leapt from their ponies and handed their reins to James and Seth. It took two men just to get Seth on to the buffalo hide saddle. 'Where'n tarnation are the stirrups,' he asked.

'We no need for white man's foot rests, use knees,' Running Tree said.

'Knees! They barely keep me up fer walkin' never mind ridin',' Seth said.

'Jus' ride, you 'onery ol' coot, and quit your mouthin'. At least we ain't dead, yet,' Jacob said, and started to walk into the blazing sunshine.

★ ★ ★

The progress was slow. The wagon lurched and bumped, seemingly hitting every rock that God created. So far, Sam thought, so good. At least I'm still alive. I've got to remain calm, got to try and figure a way of getting out of here, preferably with the aeroplane.

Burt had hardly said a word since they set off. He rode ahead, Joe just behind him. The rest of the gang just trailed to the rear. None of them spoke.

Sam had noticed one of the men behind her kept getting closer, he was looking directly at her and she didn't like the look on his face.

The driver of the wagon, who smelled as if he hadn't washed for a year, barely gave her a glance. But the ugly thug to her left was sending shivers down her back.

She had been tied to the wagon all night, but that hadn't been the reason for not sleeping, uncomfortable though it had been. She was scared to death. She'd never been in a situation anything like this, and wasn't too sure of Burt's motives. Did he kidnap her to hold for ransom? Surely not. There would be no way he could contact any of her family. They were too far away. And if he did manage to, it could be months before any ransom demand could be met. Why did he want her and the aeroplane? No good reason, that was for sure.

Her thoughts were shattered when the thug to her left leaned across and grabbed one of her breasts in his filthy hand. At the same time, he swung out of his saddle, pushed her into the back of the wagon and in a flash was lying atop her, trying to kiss her mouth.

The stench was like nothing she had experienced before. The unshaven, dirty leering face was inches from her own. She could see his black, rotting stumps that once passed for teeth. His skin was leathery, the grime so ingrained no amount of washing would ever get it off.

She felt his hand move down her body, pulling at her skirt, trying to lift it up and expose her long underwear. The shock had been so great, that she didn't struggle, at first. Realization dawned. Her worst nightmare was about to become reality.

Nobody seemed to be taking any notice. The riders to the rear had moved closer to the wagon, the driver didn't even look round. To Sam, it seemed that the other riders had formed a pre-arranged queue. A queue to rape her!

That was when she screamed.

The sound split the air. Momentarily, the would-be rapist halted in his tracks. Then a sly grin appeared in one corner of his mouth, saliva dropped from his cracked lips and landed on the side of her cheek. She retched.

She thought she'd blacked out.

Maybe she did for a second, but that was all. The next thing she was aware of was that the body on top of hers was lifted into the air and thrown from the wagon. Burt stood there, a sneer on his face, looking directly into her eyes. He seemed to be trying to make up his mind. Should he have her now, or not?

Not.

He jumped from the wagon and landed

by the side of the fallen man.

Fear shone from his eyes like a cornered animal. He got himself to his feet, backed away from Burt, then ran.

Burt seemed to enjoy that. Taking out one of his sidearms, he cocked the brim of his hat a little higher with the barrel, took a deep breath, aimed, and fired.

The running man seemed to run for a few steps more. Like a chicken who hasn't realized his head's been chopped off. The impact of the bullet spurred him on.

Then he looked down at his chest. The exit wound of the bullet had blown a hole in his shirt. So big, he could have got both fists in it. He saw the white shards of broken bone. The blood. Although he didn't know it, one of his lungs was flapping wildly as he still ran.

It was the breathing he felt first. Or rather, the lack of it. His mouth was wide open, he was sure he was yelling. But there was no sound. He couldn't breathe.

All of this he noticed in a few seconds.

Then he died.

Burt walked up to the lifeless body, and, using a foot, turned it over. He grinned into the dead man's face, then he fired again, and again and again.

The face exploded in a crimson fountain. After the third shot, the head had gone.

One eyeball, complete and intact, lay on the desert sand staring blindly at Burt. Burt lifted his boot and squashed it.

Calmly, Burt stood for a few seconds. Re-holstered his gun. Then walked slowly back to his horse, looked at Sam, and mounted.

The gang moved off in silence. Still the wagon driver didn't look at her. The riders to the rear were now much further back. The fire in their loins dissipated.

Burt had made his point.

★ ★ ★

The sun beat down unmercifully. For the riders, although uncomfortable atop the

Indians' ponies, they weren't sweating as much as the men who were walking. Jacob's boots were filling with sand. Blisters were forming. His feet were on fire. He didn't say anything though, not with these youngsters around. No way he was going to lose face.

Running Tree and Wolf Wind, true to their word, were scouting ahead. Jacob couldn't see them, but every so often a small pile of stones was set for them to follow.

Thirst. That was the biggest enemy. Jacob could already feel his lips swelling, the more he licked them, the drier they got.

They had been walking, he reckoned, for about five hours. The wagon tracks were fainter now. Here even on the fringe of the open desert, the slightest breeze moved the sand around to form little waves. Any tracks, even their own, would be covered inside of a few hours.

Jacob tried hard not to think of water. He thought of women. But not for long. The mental images of bygone conquests soon evaporated into pools of cool, clear water. No matter how hard he tried.

James was slumped forward on the pony. Conscious, just. The pain in his arm had ebbed a little to the point where he literally fell asleep in the saddle.

Lucky man, Jacob thought, *at least he won't be thinking about water.*

His brain must be dead. Jacob almost kicked himself. Cactus. They were surrounded by cactus. Some of them upwards of twenty feet high. Water. How could he have been so stupid?

'Time to stop a whiles an' take us a drink,' he said as coolly as he could.

Lewis turned to face him, his eyes shone brightly. 'You got water?'

'Nope. But these here cactuses have,' Jacob replied.

Seth was beginning to smile, slowly. 'Seems our heads are full o' horse-shit,' he said.

Jacob went to the one of the tallest cactus plants that looked more like a tree. Grabbing a petrified stick from the ground, he thrust it into the fleshy stem.

Immediately, a trickle of clear liquid started to run down the stick, dropping very slowly off the end on to the sand. Jacob placed his parched lips on the end of the stick and let the bitter-tasting liquid, the best taste he could remember, dribble into his mouth.

Quickly the rest of the party followed suit. Although it didn't taste much like water, it was wet, and as long as the tracks didn't veer off into the open desert, at least they wouldn't die of thirst.

Feeling a whole lot better, they helped James back on to the pony, but Seth decided he'd walk for a while, and Jacob hoped to high hell an' back that he would be the one to take the other pony.

He was.

Slowly the small group moved off to follow the tracks left by the Indians.

After another hour, they came across the body. They couldn't recognize who it was, except they knew it wasn't Burt. The buzzards had already begun their grisly task of picking at the soft exposed flesh. Lewis was the first one to throw up.

The birds only tolerated the interruption to their meal for a few minutes, then they began to get braver, squawking and fighting amongst themselves, edging nearer their dinner, trying to get the interlopers out of the way so they could pick the carcass clean.

'Ain't no point in tryin' to bury that mess,' Seth stated. 'Might jus' as well leave it where it is.'

'Don' think we got the energy to do much at the moment anyways,' Jacob answered.

'That's the worst sight I ever seen,' James said. 'Jus' look at his head!'

'Yeah, well, let's get a move on, they can't be too far ahead.' Jacob dug his heels into the pony's flanks and moved off at walking pace, followed by James and the rest.

'What the hell we gonna do when we do sight 'em?' Seth said. 'We ain't exactly in a fightin' state at the moment.'

'Yeah, well, we'll jus' have to play it by ear, I guess. Them In'ians may come up wi' somethin', Jacob said. 'I sure as hell can't think straight yet.' They went on in silence.

★ ★ ★

Running Tree and Wolf Wind were close, they could smell their quarry, even though as yet they couldn't see them. The creaking wagon-wheels could faintly be heard in the distance. They looked to their rear. The sky, brilliant blue, showed the buzzards that were still arriving at the body they'd discovered. They assumed that by now, the rest of their party would at least be near, or even at, the scene of the shooting.

Both men kept running, for it was not by chance that they had been given their names.

Within an hour, they caught their first glimpse of the wagon. They could see Sam sitting on the duck-board, so they knew that, for the time being, she was safe. The day was wearing on; pretty soon, darkness would paint the desert black. Then they would camp. That

111

would be the time to strike, they knew. But in the darkness, many things can go wrong. Indian war culture was embedded in their minds from many nights of listening to the old men on the Reservation recalling their battles. Always in the light, never at night.

Silently, as only Indians can, they followed the wagon until it stopped by the side of a dried up arroya. Now was the time to return to their party. A battle plan must be drawn up.

Arriving back, Running Tree and Wolf Wind stroked their ponies. The affiliation between Indian and pony is strong, and although the ponies had tolerated their new masters they were getting edgy with unease.

'Nice to see you two boys again,' Seth said by way of welcome.

'Any sign of them yet? Did you see Sam? Is she OK?' James blurted.

'The answer to all three questions is the one yes. They have stopped for the night by an old river bed, not more than thirty of your minutes from here.' Running Tree squatted on the ground.

'Now all we got to figure is how in the hell we tackle 'em. All-out attack ain't no good. We're too weak still, an' we ain't enough armoury for that,' Jacob said.

'Night would be best,' suggested Lewis. 'Sneak up on 'em and kill 'em while they sleep,'

'Night not good. Mistakes can be made,' Wolf Wind offered.

'Mebbe dawn then,' Seth questioned, 'catch 'em in the light afore they wake.'

'Might well be, might well be,' pondered Jacob. 'What we need to do is git as close as possible afore nightfall. 'Course, that means it's gonna be a long, cold night, but we need all our strength back, an', speaking for myself, I ain't nowheres near that yet.'

'Agreed.' James dropped from the back of the pony, wincing slightly as the jar from his legs reached his wounded arm. 'I think a sneak attack at first light, rescue Sam and the aeroplane and hightail it outta here.'

'We go get water now,' said Wolf Wind.

'Where in the hell you gonna get that?' Lewis asked.

'We know when we know,' Running Tree said.

'Well, we got two empty canteens here, if you can, you might fill 'em for us.' Seth passed over the two canteens.

'Keep following our signs, at large rock, camp for night. We can light fire there,' Wolf Wind said.

'If'n we light a fire they're sure to see the smoke,' Lewis said.

'Indian fires don't make smoke.' For the first time that day, Brad spoke. 'Besides, if there's a large rock there, nobody'll see any flame, either.'

'My, my, you're a dark horse, ain't ya,' Seth said grinning. 'Beginning to think you was mute, or some-thin'.'

'Talk when it's necessary. Listen mostly,' Brad answered.

'We go now,' Running Tree said and both Indians disappeared.

It took almost exactly half an hour to reach the large rock. Tethering the two Indian ponies, Jacob and James joined the others behind it. If somebody had tried to chisel out a kitchen stove out of the large rock, they wouldn't have made any better job than Mother Nature.

At the base of the rock was a recess with what looked like a small chimney. Brad was right, their quarry wouldn't even see the flames.

Running Tree and Wolf Wind returned. Not only were the canteens full of cool, but sandy water, they had also captured some lizards and a snake.

The fire lit, the food cooked and eaten, a last mouthful of water, and the party settled down for the night. All that is except Running Tree, who took first watch. He would awaken Lewis next, who in turn would pass the watch over to Seth, and so on.

Jacob lay back on the still warm sand near the fire and stared at the darkening sky. Once the sun dropped below the mountain line, the darkness would be total. Vaguely, he began to pick out the stars as, one by one, they became stronger. There was no moon. He fell asleep.

9

Jacob's eyes opened the moment his shoulder was shaken. Seth was at his side, Running Tree and Wolf Wind by him. It was pitch black and freezing cold.

'You looked awful purty asleep there, almost a shame to wake you up,' Seth said.

'Darned ol' fool,' Jacob said as he tried to sit up, failed, tried again and rested on one elbow.

'Sun will be up soon. Camp still there, all sleeping.' Wolf Wind said.

'Give me a minute to come to, why don't you,' Jacob said standing. 'I gotta take a leak first afore I do anythin' as sobering as thinkin'.' With that, he disappeared into the night. But they could hear him.

Lewis relit the fire and they all huddled round its meagre warmth.

'I don't think there's much I can do to help,' James said.

'I made me a spear, so at least it'll be quiet.' Seth said. 'We got two knives, so we should keep the gunfire to a minimum at first else we'll be outnumbered and outgunned.'

'What I reckon is we surround their campsite, then, one o' the In'ians gets in the camp and finds out where Sam is, so's she can be kept safe. That way when the shootin' starts she ain't gonna get accidentally shot,' Lewis began.

'I knewed it, you open your mouth often enough somethin' sensible was bound to get out,' Seth said.

'Seems like a good enough plan to me,' Jacob said. 'But I reckon James here, if'n you feel up to it, son, should go in first and quieten down Miss Sam.'

'Sure I can do that, with pleasure,' beamed James.

'That's what I reckoned, son, that's what I reckoned,' Jacob continued. 'Right, Hank, Brad and Running Tree, if'n you take the far side, me an' Seth an' Lewis here as well as Wolf Wind, will come from the south. James, you stick close by an' give us a signal when you've found Sam. OK?'

'OK!' they chorused.

Silently, or as silently as they could, they set off to surround Burt's campsite.

A cold, grey light had started up in the east, they knew that within the next fifteen to twenty minutes the sun would appear over the distant mountains. So whatever happened would have to happen now.

They approached the sleeping figures, who formed a circle round the now dead camp-fire. They were indistinguishable. James slipped into the campsite and, under the guidance of Wolf Wind, made for the sleeping figure of Sam, tied beneath a tarp on the wagon.

They waited. James roused Sam, putting his good hand over her mouth as she awoke to save the inevitable scream. As soon as she saw James, tears welled in her eyes and if she had been able, she would have shouted with joy. But James kept his hand firmly over her mouth. When he was sure she would be silent, he removed his hand, placed one finger to lips to indicate silence, and then cooed.

The sound reached the waiting men and slowly they crept towards the sleeping figures. Running Tree got there first and with a loud shriek he plunged his knife deep into the nearest figure.

Unfortunately, the rest of the men were about ten seconds behind him. In that time the Indian's shriek woke the rest of the party.

It was too late now for stealth. Jacob and Seth dropped to the ground, Seth, armed only with a make-do spear, Jacob with his gun.

The first shots rang out, shattering the early morning stillness. Hank was hit full in the chest by a double-barrelled shotgun. His chest exploded as he was lifted off his feet and propelled backwards a full ten feet.

Brad dropped to his knees, then fell face first into the dirt without even loosening off a shot. The side of Brad's head was missing.

Meantime, Running Tree and Lewis

had taken care of two more of the gang before they beat a hasty retreat to the relative safety of the surrounding rocks.

'Shit!' Jacob whispered. What in the hell do we do now? We don' even know how many there are.'

'Wisht I had ma gun with me,' Seth said.

'I'm kinda glad you ain't, otherwise more of us might get killed,' Jacob countered.

'Where'd that kid Lewis get to?' Jacob asked Seth.

'Soon as the damned fool Indian yelled he ran in. Luck was with him though, as the sleepers all turned towards Running Tree, I saw him get one before he ran off.'

Burt was crouched near the fire. The amount of shooting had subsided, with that, he assumed, the men who had attacked his camp were either low on ammo or, and the thought brought a smile to his lips, they didn't all have guns.

He'd hit two men, one with the shotgun, the other with his Colt, a lucky shot, but they all counted. The woman. He must get to the woman. An' how come she hadn't started in a yelling? Ah, someone's there with her. Keeping her safe and quiet.

Well he'd see about that.

Crawling on his belly, he crept towards the wagon, the rest of his men were still firing blindly into the early morning greyness. Fools, he thought, no brains between 'em. But he more'n made up for that.

Nearing the wagon, he saw two figures, one with a hat on. Taking careful aim, he fired off three shots. The hat danced away under the wagon, and he heard a stifled scream.

So, he may have hit one of 'em, or both. Or the hat was a trick, yes, that was it, the hat was probably on a rock to fool him. Well, he weren't no fool.

He crept closer. All around him gunfire, but none was being returned. He heard panicked breathing. Knew it was the woman. He listened, only one set of breathing. Again he grinned.

As soon as the Indian yelled, James grabbed Sam and pushed her roughly to the floor. He knew that lead would be flying, and he didn't want her hit. He'd hardly had a chance to get to know her, and he sure did want to do that. Even under the heavy gunfire, he couldn't help thinking how beautiful she was.

He pulled her backwards, underneath the wagon, removed his hat and placed it on a rock, might gain him a bit of time, he thought.

As the third shot hit the hat, the bullet ricocheted off the rock beneath it and slew across his forehead, breaking the skin, but not the bone. The force was such that it knocked him out cold.

Sam thought he was dead. She'd put her hand to his head and it came back covered in blood. She wanted to scream. She wanted to run but she couldn't. She knew that if she so much as moved, whoever had killed James would almost certainly kill her. She waited. Trying to stop her heart racing.

The men in the campsite were so busy shooting their weapons off that they didn't notice they weren't being shot at. They hadn't time to see if any of their number had been hit, not that they would have cared less.

They spread themselves out a bit further, seeking cover when and how they could. Chas found a body and crouched down behind it. He wasn't sure where the attack was coming from, but he sure as hell didn't want to die without taking someone with him. The more the merrier.

Lying perfectly still, he squinted into the morning light, trying to make out any signs of movement. Nothing moved. Raising his head slightly to get a better view he caught a glimpse of something shiny just as the knife reached his throat.

Wolf Wind was lying the other side of the dead body. Just waiting for an opportunity. The opportunity came. Chas tried to shout but the only sound that came out of his throat was a blood-curdling gurgle.

He struggled to his feet and immediately he was hit in the kneecap by a bullet. One of his own men, mistaking him for an attacker, just let loose.

Chas fell back to earth, blood pumping from his jugular in an arc covering Wolf Wind from head to toe. But Wolf Wind just waited.

Gradually, Chas ceased all movement. He twitched once, and the leg that had almost been severed by the impact of the bullet was the last to go.

Carefully, Wolf Wind crept towards the dead body of Chas and, with little effort, removed his scalp. Tucking it into his belt, only just containing his pleasure at winning his first battle trophy, he lay in wait behind the barrier of now two dead bodies.

* * *

Burt kept still. Listened and moved forward, snakelike. There she was. The first rays of the sunlight were tracing their way across the plains, giving enough of a backdrop for him to make out her head and shoulders.

He could see her profile as well as that of the body next to her. So, he had hit one them after all. He crept forward. Sam stared straight ahead hoping to catch sight of her adversary.

In the darkness Sam couldn't see anything. The light was behind her but not strong enough. She knew someone was out there, but who? James was dead. All the others may be for all she knew.

What to do?

She started reaching out with her hands, looking for James's gun. She didn't find it. James was unarmed.

Burt slipped round the side of the wagon and Sam felt hands on the back of her neck. She didn't know anything about it. Quickly, Burt gathered her up in his arms and carried her to where they'd corralled the horses the night before. Still with their saddles on, they had treated their animals with the same degree of thought and respect as they treated everyone else. None.

Burt threw the rag-like figure of Sam across a horse, reached out for the lariat tied to the pommel and firmly strapped her on.

Taking the reins, he gathered another horse to him and led them both out into desert. Behind him the gunfire was now sporadic, but enough to let him know that they were busy enough not to know what he was up to.

He escaped.

Light began to paint the scene. Seth could make out Wolf Wind, lying just ahead of him. He couldn't make out much else yet, but it wouldn't be long before it would be bright enough. He looked to his left and right. He and Jacob needed some cover. The sparse clump of grass they were hiding behind wouldn't stop cow piss.

They began to crawl to their left to a pile of rocks, barely big enough for one to hide behind, let alone two.

Shots were ringing out from around the camp, Seth and Jacob were more worried about being hit by their own people than anything else. At long last they reached the relative safety of the rocks, each of them breathing a sigh of relief.

'What now, pardner?' Seth whispered.

'Seems like we're stuck,' Jacob replied.

'Light's comin'. I can make out two, one to the left of the fire, one to the right. An' look, ain't that Lewis there way back? Running Tree must be near him. Can't see James, though. What in the hell's happened to him, an' where's Sam?' Seth was getting agitated.

'Looks like two of the boys got hit there. They ain't movin', can't quite make out who,' Jacob said straining his eyes in the half-light.

A bullet hit the rock in front of them, Jacob let off a volley, careful to keep his shots low, he didn't want to hit Lewis and Running Tree if he could help it.

From the other side of the camp, Lewis fired at the muzzle flashes he'd seen. He still couldn't tell if he hit anything or not. Running Tree was aware of Jacob and Seth, he motioned Lewis to follow him. Stealthily, they crawled backwards and round to eventually join up with the old-timers.

'Did you see any sign of James?' Jacob asked.

'No, not a thing,' Lewis replied. 'Sun's shining directly in our eyes, Running Tree was afraid we might hit you by mistake. That's why we've moved round.'

'Where did you last see Sam,' Seth enquired.

'Beneath wagon,' Running Tree replied.

'Then we must assume that, dead or alive, that's where James is.' Seth began to edge out from behind the rocks. Immediately a shot rang out. It missed, but Seth moved back behind cover quicker than he'd ever moved before in his life.

'Goddamn! Seems they got us pinned down here,' Seth said.

'No kiddin', you ever thought of bein' a Pinkerton?' Jacob replied sarcastically.

'Sun's almost up, we'll have to try and see how many there are and where they are,' Lewis said. 'How many guns we got?'

'I've got one, an' you've got one,' Jacob said, 'That's it.'

'Well that ain't enough,' Seth groaned. 'An' where the hell's Wolf Wind?'

'My brother is yonder, lying by those bodies, near the camp-fire,' Running Tree said. 'I'll call him.'

With that, Running Tree made a bird-like sound. Wolf Wind, without moving his lower body, turned his head to indicate he was all right. The light was much brighter now and Running Tree could see his brother quite clearly, he motioned with his hand to indicate a gun, Wolf Wind nodded that he understood.

Moving stealthily, Wolf Wind edged sideways. The bodies in front of him must have had guns, he just had to find them. Reaching round the front of the nearest body, he felt for the holster. Empty. He untied the belt-buckle and removed it. The belt was laden with bullets. It was a start. Holding the belt in his left hand, he threw it backwards, where it landed within inches of Running Tree's outstretched fingers.

Again, shots rang out. Obviously they had been spotted, as had the gunbelt.

Carefully, Wolf Wind manoeuvred himself further to the right. He saw the gun, lying in the dust. Gently, he edged forward, managing to get one finger on the trigger guard, he pulled it towards him. Safely held, he tossed the gun in the direction of the gunbelt.

Running Tree retrieved both belt and gun. Now they had three guns and enough ammunition, possibly.

Wolf Wind held up four fingers and pointed to his right. Running Tree understood. 'There are four men. There.' He pointed the direction for the others.

We got t' flush 'em out, somehow,' Seth said, loading his weapon.

'We need to spread out from here in a line,' Jacob said. 'Running Tree, see if you can get your brother to act as a decoy. If he can make a dash to the wagon, drawing their fire, Seth an' me can cover him, while you two move to the left there, Lewis, and you to the right, behind those other rocks. That way we can catch 'em in the crossfire.'

Running Tree nodded in agreement, using his hands only, Running Tree indicated to Wolf Wind the plan. He seemed to understand for he nodded. Then, raising himself to his knees, he indicated he was going for the wagon.

'Right, git ready, we may only have one chance,' Jacob said.

At Running Tree's signal, Wolf Wind moved like lightning towards the wagon. Immediately, Lewis and Running Tree broke left and right. Seth and Jacob set up a volley of covering fire hoping to keep the four men pinned down. It almost worked.

★ ★ ★

Burt looked over his shoulder. There was no sign of anyone following. He'd heard sporadic gunfire, then silence. Samantha was still unconscious. Good. Plenty of time to wake her up, he thought. Mebbe I'll take her this time, show her what a real man's made of. He chuckled to himself. Reaching into his coat pocket, he retrieved a half-smoked cheroot and, without trying to light it, wedged it in the corner of his mouth.

He knew this area. To the outsider it was open land, where the prairie met the desert. But Burt knew a hundred hiding places, used most of them at one time or another. There was water, too, at some of the places so he wasn't worried. He'd survive and take pleasure in the woman as often as he wanted with no interference.

It was a pity about the aeroplane, he thought. Could have used that right enough. No posse in the world could follow that thing. No tracks, quick getaway. It would have been a dream come true. Maybe it still would, after all, he still had the woman.

There was a groan behind him. Samantha was coming to. He gave her no more than a cursory glance. She was bound and gagged, there was nothing she could do. He grinned to himself again.

James was in a daze. His head throbbed and he fought to remember where he was and what he was doing there. Then he remembered Sam.

He felt a strange feeling in his stomach. He didn't know what it was, but it had started the moment he thought of Sam.

He'd never felt this way before. Even the wound to his head had stopped throbbing and a warm glow seemed to envelop his body. Maybe, he thought, it was the bump on the head that was making him feel this way.

Then Sam's face appeared in his mind's eye and realization hit him. He was in love.

James raised himself up on one elbow and surveyed the scene around him. He became aware of sporadic gunshots. He tried to sit up but banged his head on the underside of the wagon.

★ ★ ★

'Yessiree, life is on the up,' Burt said out loud. 'You an' me, little lady, are gonna be famous. We're a gonna swoop into town, rob the bank and swoop right on out again. No one's ever gonna be able to get us. Me doin' the robbin' an' you the flyin'. What a team!'

★ ★ ★

The first bullet caught Wolf Wind in the heel. It didn't stop him though, he still made a rush for the wagon. The bullet tore his heel off just below the ankle. He didn't feel any pain. The second bullet caught him in the back, to the left of his spine. The wound still shattered his spine like a twig. Again he felt no pain. He felt nothing. He hit the dirt and didn't move. Ever again.

At the sound of the shooting, James came to. For a second he couldn't remember where he was or what he'd been doing. Then it came to him in a hurry. He felt his forehead. It was sore, but the bleeding had stopped. He'd have a nice scar as a trophy.

He saw Wolf Wind running towards him. Saw the explosion as the first bullet blew his foot off. Saw the second. James closed his eyes as the Indian fell to the ground.

The gunfire continued. He caught sight of Lewis, thank God he was OK, he thought to himself. Wearily, he moved his head and saw Seth and Jacob, it would seem that nothing could get those two. He understood now what they were doing.

From his vantage point, he could see the four desperados quite clearly. They obviously hadn't seen him. He reached for his holster, but he remembered he'd given his gun to Jacob. What now?

He began to crawl from beneath the wagon. Seth and Jacob were still firing, so the attention was on them. Lewis, now safe behind some rocks, began firing also. The four men ducked down under the rain of bullets. One got hit in the ear, the force of the shell sending him flying backwards. In his defenceless state, it was easy for Lewis to finish him off.

Now only three men. The odds were getting better.

James reached towards the buckboard, hoping like hell no one had seen him move. There in the footwell was a shotgun, a crumpled box of shells next to it. Slowly he lifted the gun and brought it to him. Carefully placing it on the floor, he reached in and got the shell box too. Now he was armed. But he was only one-armed.

Breaking the shotgun wasn't an easy thing to do with one good arm, but he made it, loaded it, and took aim. He knew the spread from this distance was wide, he also knew that it would inflict more pain than injury. But it sure would give the three men something to think about.

Resting the barrel of the shotgun on the side of the wagon, he took careful aim and fired both barrels. The screams from the three men filled the air. James was right. They weren't badly injured, but they sure were hurting.

All three men forgot in their pain that to the front of them were shooters. They all as one stood holding arms and legs and backsides. Seth, Jacob and Lewis had a turkey shoot.

Within seconds the three men were cut down and out of their misery. Silence reigned.

After a couple of minutes, James came out from behind the wagon, sure there was no more danger. Seth and Jacob stood up, Lewis and Running Tree ran into the campsite. Lewis to make sure James was all right, Running Tree to realize his worst fears. In two days he had lost two brothers.

They covered the bodies of Hank and Brad. Lewis was in tears. He seemed to have known the two all his life. They were more like brothers than friends.

James tried to console him, but he felt the same way, so they hugged each other. Seth started collecting rocks and gently laid them on the bodies. James broke off and joined in. Lewis stood for moment, then helped.

'Somebody should say a few words,' Lewis said. 'We can't just not say anythin'.'

'We said it in our minds, Lewis, none of us here are church-going folks. But I'll say a few words if'n you like.' Seth cleared his throat.

'Lord, now you take real good care o' these boys. I guess you know 'em better'n I do, but they seemed OK to me. Amen.'

The small group dispersed. James frantically searched the campsite. There was no sign of Samantha. Worse, there was no sign of Burt.

'Damn! Looks like it still ain't over,' James said. 'Burt and Sam ain't here.'

'Then we go on,' Seth said as he looked over the dead bodies.

'Sure is a mess,' Lewis said. 'Never killed nobody before.'

'It was you or them, son,' Jacob consoled him. 'These scum-bags ain't worth the time of day.'

' 'Spose we'll have to bury 'em first, huh?' Lewis said.

'Can't leave 'em like this, son. Move

'em all together and cover 'em with rocks's all we can do now,' Seth said wearily.

Their thoughts were interrupted by the chanting coming from Running Tree. The four men had forgotten his loss. Seth walked over to the prostrate figure of Running Tree and placed his hand on his shoulder.

'We ain't known you too long, but we kinda figure you're one of us now. I'm sorry for your loss, boy. Real sorry.'

'Now I have no brothers. Both are dead.' Running Tree was in tears. For the first time in his life, he was alone. 'My mother and father were killed by the blue-coats while we were on our way to the Reservation. The bluecoats were meant to escort us, but they had whiskey. They got drunk and wanted women. Any women would do. They raped my mother, and when my father went to her aid, they shot him like a dog. When they had finished with my mother, she was already dead. I saw a white man rape my dead mother. I was too young to help.'

'Jesus H. Christ, boy.' Seth could think of nothing else to say.

Running Tree picked up the dead body of his brother and walked out of the campsite. Seth could neither do or say anything. He'd seen plenty in his life, heard a lot more. But the grief he saw in this Indian's face touched him.

Jacob and Lewis, who had managed to control his feeling of the need to throw up, had dragged the bodies to the side of the campsite, and were busy gathering rocks to cover them. James, whose arm was feeling much better, but whose head really ached, sat and watched.

'How far do you think he's got with her?' he asked Seth.

'In the desert? Not far, if'n that's what you mean, James,' Seth replied.

'That's exactly what I mean,' said James.

'Now we've got guns, food, water and ammo, not to mention horses, we'll soon track him down,' Jacob offered.

'But he's still got Sam. It ain't gonna be that easy,' Lewis said.

'No. No one said it was gonna be easy,' Seth said.

'Some of us should stay here and guard the camp and aeroplane, I think I should be the one who goes after Burt,' James said.

'I think you may have an objection to that, son,' Jacob motioned towards Running Tree. 'We had us an agreement. I can't see Running Tree letting you get at Burt.'

'Then Running Tree and I should go after him.

He can take Burt, I just want to save Sam.' James looked round the others.

'Well, son, I reckon if'n that's what you want, that's what you got. Seth an' me ain't no good in a gunfight anyways, an' these ol' bones get t' creaking even when I take a crap. Let's put it to Running Tree,' said Jacob.

Running Tree agreed. They knew he would. But first he had to honour the spirit of his dead brother. They all offered to help, but he refused it. Only an Indian can bury an Indian.

After coffee that tasted like nectar to Seth and Jacob, they chewed on hardtack and biscuits for a while, being the only food any of them had eaten in the last two days, even though they had precious little appetite.

Lewis collected all the guns and ammunition together and picked out the best horse for James. James was moving his arm, flexing his fingers, trying by some miracle to get it working. They packed the saddle-bags with some of the biscuits and hardtack, and made sure their canteens were full.

'We'll wait here three days. If'n you ain't back in that time, we'll figure you ain't comin' back,' said Jacob.

'Fair enough. Lewis, if'n I don't come back, you make sure Ma and Pa know. OK?' James put his hand on Lewis's shoulder.

'Hell, I aim to come with you, James,' Lewis pleaded.

'No you ain't. One of us has got to get back an' tell our folks.'

Running Tree slowly led his pony out

of the campsite, he didn't look back. Seth and Jacob shook James's hand and wished them luck.

They'd need it.

10

The sun beat down unmercifully. There wasn't, nor had there been, a cloud in the sky for days now.

Burt was used to being uncomfortable, he'd been uncomfortable all his life. But Samantha was a different story.

They had been riding now for six hours, from their rude awakening just before dawn in the coldness of the desert night. Now, the heat was almost unbearable.

It wasn't so much the ropes that hurt. Sam had been tied to the horse over the saddle face down. Her stomach really hurt from the jostling about on the unforgiving leather. The left side of her face was sore from the continual rubbing of the stirrup straps and, although her hair had fallen over her face, protecting it from the sun, her neck was bare.

She could feel the skin shrinking and burning and there wasn't a damn thing she could do about it. She'd heard about sunstroke, it now looked as if she was going to experience it.

She was thirsty. So thirsty. The gag in her mouth was drying her tongue and lips far quicker than the sun could ever have done. She tried to attract Burt's attention, but he seemed in a world of his own.

Burt indeed was. He was planning a whole series of bank robberies. Swooping down out of the sky, grabbing the money, then off again into the blue yonder. The very thought of it was giving him a hard-on.

Sam groaned louder. 'What the hell you want, woman,' he spat over his shoulder. 'You an' me's gonna get rich, very rich.'

Sam groaned again.

Burt halted the lead horse and swivelled round in the saddle. He looked at her proud backside that was facing him and licked his lips. Not yet, pretty lady, he thought, and not right here, but pretty damn soon.

'What d'you want?' he sneered. 'You want some o' this?' and he cupped his balls with his hand and laughed. 'Well, like it or not, you're gonna get some real soon.'

He led his horse round to face Sam. He looked at the slim line of her exposed neck, and although he noticed it was very red, that's not what he was thinking about.

'You an' me, gal, you an' me.' He seemed to think this hilarious and he rocked back and forth in his saddle.

Sam uttered one word. 'AUGHTTERR.'

'What? What's that you say?' Burt leaned closer.

'Aughterr,' Sam struggled with the word.

'Oughtta what? What the hell you tryin' t' say?' Burt laughed again. 'Seems like I'll have to take your gag off, li'l lady, now you can rant and rave as much as you want, but there ain't no one but me to hear you, an' as soon as I get fed up with your hollerin' I'll jus' gag you up agin, got that?'

Sam nodded furiously.

'Well, hold still now.' Burt leant forward and untied the stinking neck cloth he'd tied round her mouth. Sam spat it out.

'Now what were you a tryin' to say.'

'Water. Please let me have some water. I can't escape from you, so could you please untie the ropes.' Sam's throat and mouth were much worse than she thought, the words coming out in a croak.

'Sure thing, purty lady, sure thing. Ain't used t' none o' this po-lite conversation, an' seein' as how you asked so nicely, it'll be a pleasure.'

Burt dismounted and began untying the ropes. When he'd finished, he lifted Sam down by the waist, turned her around and looked her full in the face.

'You an' me are gonna make sweet music tonight, li'l lady, you can bet your life on that. As soon as we pitch camp I'm gonna show you a real man.' Burt forced her body against his.

'Yes, sure, anything you say, but please,

can I have some water?' Sam said.

Burt went to his horse and unhooked the canteen. Unscrewing the top he handed it to her. 'Don' drink too much or too quickly, else you'll be ill,' he cautioned.

The water tasted awful. But she drank, then poured a little on to her hand and rubbed the back of her neck. She winced at the pain.

'Goddamn it to hell, woman. Don't you go wastin' water,' Burt slapped the side of her face with such force that, in her weakened state, it sent her flying.

'An' don't drop that canteen, neither,' he shouted down at her.

Sam got to her feet, canteen still in hand. 'I'm sorry, I didn't think. My neck's badly burnt, I-I just wanted to ease it.'

Burt bent forward and picked up the neck cloth he'd used to gag her. 'Here, tie this roun' your neck, it'll stop it gettin' any more burnt.'

Sam felt relieved, she thought he was about to bind and gag her once more.

'Thank you.' She slipped the neck cloth on.

Burt turned and remounted his horse. 'Come on, mount up. Places to go, people to rob,' he laughed.

Sam struggled up on the horse. It was a big mare, much bigger than she'd ever ridden before and it took all her strength just to get in the saddle.

They rode on.

★ ★ ★

James had been following Running Tree, but now he pulled up alongside. 'I'm sorry about, you know, your brothers an' all. I didn' git to know 'em none too well, but, well, you know.' James ran out of words. Running Tree acknowledged his comments with a nod of the head.

'I kill Burt,' was all he said.

'You sure will, pardner, you sure will.'

They rode on in silence for a while. Even talking made you break out in a sweat. Except that Running Tree didn't sweat. Didn't seem too hot at all.

James removed his hat and wiped the inside brim with a bandanna, trying to dry out the sweat that had stained it over the years.

The tracks they were following were still easily visible. Two horses heading west. Although Running Tree didn't know the terrain, it held no fears for him. He could find water should the need arise, and there was plenty to eat, even in the desert, if you knew where to look.

James was more apprehensive. Thankful that Running Tree was there. He'd been brought up in a small township, knew nothing of the wilderness. He knew that without Running Tree he'd be as good as dead.

* * *

Seth was in good spirits. He'd got plenty of hot steaming black coffee in front of him bubbling away on the open campfire, food in his belly and somewhere comfortable to lie down in out of the glaring sun's heat.

What more could a man ask for? When he felt like it, he was going to root through the wagon and see what he could find. The aeroplane was firmly tied on to the flat-back, easy enough to transport, hopefully with Sam back alive and well.

Jacob was sleeping and Lewis was keeping an eye on the territory. He'd climbed a small hillock and, rifle in hand, stood staring at the desert.

Seth closed his eyes and began to nap. Underneath the wagon was cool in comparison and with Lewis keeping a look-out, sleep came over him.

The shot rang out and Seth was almost deafened by it. Sitting bolt upright, something he hadn't been able to do for many a year, he banged his head on the underside of the wagon. Not enough to deck him, but sure enough to hurt like hell.

Jacob stood in front of him, Colt in his hand, still smoking.

'What the hell d'you think you're playin' at,' Seth growled.

Without a word, Jacob stepped forward, picked up the dead snake by its hollow tail, and dropped it on Seth's lap. 'Present for you.'

He turned and walked back to the camp-fire to get a cup of coffee.

'You might've woken me up first,' Seth shouted after him.

'Snake woulda done that, all right, sank his fangs in your fat ol' head sure enough. You must a disturbed it with your goddamned snoring,' Jacob shouted back.

'I don' damn well snore,' Seth was indignant.

'Well you sure as hell make a good attempt,' Jacob said sipping the boiling brew.

'What's goin' on? Who fired the shot off?' Lewis said as he came running into the campsite.

'Nothin' to worry your pretty little head about, son,' Jacob said. 'Seems like Seth there fell asleep in the same place as a rattler. I had a split second to decide which one to shoot, missed Seth.'

★ ★ ★

Burt felt hungry. In the rush to sneak out under the hail of bullets, he'd only brought water, and not much of that. He felt like eating now though. It was still two or three hours away from his first hiding place, food stored there in case of an emergency. And there had been plenty of them in his life.

His thoughts, though, were concerned more with Sam. He'd had plenty of women in his life. Some he'd paid for. Some were willing. Some were not.

Now whether she'd be willing in the end made no difference to Burt. One way or another, he was going to have her.

'I sure can't wait to get to our first stop, li'l lady, I'm gonna sure show you a good time. Yessiree.' His laughter sent a chill down Sam's spine.

'What makes you think that?' Sam said.

'I know you can't resist a real man.' Burt was serious. 'I'm gonna have you beggin' me not to stop.'

'How much further is it then?' Sam asked.

'See, you can hardly wait. Shouldn't be more'n two or three hours at most.' Burt had dropped back and was now riding beside Sam.

With the tip of his rifle, he began to lift up her long skirt. Trying to take a peek at what was underneath.

Sam decided to play it cool. She didn't want to upset this man. She'd seen what he was capable of. Her only thoughts were keeping him calm, and hoping that Seth and Jacob, and anybody else, might come to her rescue. Soon.

'Now you don't want to spoil a surprise, do you?' she teased.

'Goddamn, I knew you wanted it as much as I do,' Burt said.

'Surely you're man enough to wait two or three hours?' she hoped.

'Ma'am I can wait for you, hot-diggedy-dog.' Burt replaced the rifle in its sheath, took his hat off, whooped, and sent his horse into a gallop.

Sam reined her horse in, trying to decide if she should make a break for it. Certain that his brains were between his legs, she wasn't certain how far he'd gallop off.

Burt reined in, stopped and looked round. The mere fact that Sam hadn't tried to escape, only made his ego soar even higher. He cantered back to her.

'This'll be the longest three hours you ever waited,' Burt said. His demonic laughter seemed to echo everywhere.

They rode on in silence.

★ ★ ★

Running Tree jumped from his pony. On the ground was a wad of cloth. He picked it, smelled it, then dropped it again. The sand showed that the horses had stopped. Two people, one heavy, the other light, had stood here face to face. To his left he saw the indentation in the sand where Sam had landed.

'They fight here, woman knocked over. Then stand up and get back on horse. Water spilled,'

Running Tree said in a crouched position.

'You can tell all that?' James enquired.

'See, marks in sand still fresh.'

'Was the girl hurt?'

'Difficult to say, but she got up on her own. Footprints of heavy one do not approach.'

'So they have water then?'

'Yes.'

'How far ahead?'

'Not sure. Maybe one, two hours.' Running Tree stood and seemed to be smelling the air.

'What're you doin' now?' James asked.

'Man Burt, stink. Not human being like you. I smell him soon.'

With that Running Tree jumped on his pony.

James got the canteen out and took a sip of water. 'Drink?' he asked Running Tree.

'Thank you, no. I drink later.'

The two men resumed their tracking.

'Have you figured out yet how we're gonna tackle this?' James asked.

'No. We decide when we find. Burt man, he die slowly.'

'Night time might be best,' James said.

'Yes,' was all Running Tree said.

The two men rode on in silence.

Another hour passed. Then another. Running Tree dismounted, and crouched. He had found the place where Burt had galloped off.

'What is it?' James asked in a whisper.

'One horse stop, the other go that way, then returns.'

'What in the hell for?'

'Not know.'

'Are there still two horses?'

'Yes. Both with riders.'

'How far now?'

Running Tree stood, sniffed the air. 'Soon. We wait here 'til nightfall.'

'Here? There's no shelter or anything.'

'Soon the sun will sink. Then we move.' Running Tree reached into his bed-roll and pulled out a branch.

'What now?' James asked.

Without replying, Running Tree sank the small branch into the sand. Unwrapping his bed-roll, he placed it over the branch to form a small tent.

He stood up and spread his hands. 'We rest here.'

James dismounted, tethered his horse and crawled into the tent. Running Tree joined him. Although it was hot inside, it took the late glare and heat out of the sun. They both waited.

★ ★ ★

James was rudely wakened by Running Tree. Rubbing his eyes, he saw that it was almost dark outside.

'How long did I sleep?'

'Not long. We go now.'

Packing up the bed-roll, James mounted his horse, but Running Tree led his.

'You not ridin'?' James asked.

'No. Follow tracks easier on foot.'

James jumped off his horse and followed. The night air, still warm from the blazing sun, was as quiet as the tomb. Even as they walked, both men felt the air cool down. It didn't seem possible to James, after the blazing temperatures of the daytime, that as soon as the sun dipped below the horizon, the temperature dropped in a matter of minutes.

'They are near. Hear voices,' Running Tree said as he stopped and cocked his ear in the direction of the sound that only he could hear.

'How far off?' James asked in a whisper, he didn't want to give the game away. As far as he was concerned, they still had the element of surprise, though Burt would have to be stupid if he thought that no one would try and rescue Sam.

'Other side of dune. Smell smoke. Wait here.'

With that, Running Tree disappeared into the blackness. James was left holding the reins of both horses, neither of which he could see properly.

Running Tree, unseen, crept up the side of the dune. At the top he paused. Listening to the sounds of the crackling fire. Smelling the coffee that was obviously being made. He wanted to be absolutely sure of the direction he needed to go.

He was ashamed of his behaviour at the old campsite when they had surprised Burt and his men. It was his first kill, and he lost his head. Fear had gripped his belly, and the only way to overcome that fear was to yell, and yell as loud as he knew how. But that had given them away. He knew that. He felt responsible for his elder brother's death. Now he was avenging it. The man Burt would not see daylight as a free man.

He waited and listened. Now he was sure of the direction. He cupped his hands and, scooping up a pile of sand, he made a marker, then he moved along to his left. He waited, listened, and made another marker.

Sliding back down the dune, he returned to James.

'Other side of dune. Campsite. Fire burning. I have made two markers at top of dune. You go to the one on your left, I go to right one.'

'Did you hear anythin'?' James asked.

'Only one voice. Burt's voice.'

'You think Sam's still alive?'

'We soon find out.' With that Running Tree led the way to the top of the dune. James, Winchester in his hand, followed.

Once in position, Running Tree told James what he was going to do.

'You stay here. Train rifle on camp-fire. When you hear my signal, shoot into the fire. This will distract Burt and I will do rest.'

'What's the signal?' James wanted to know. 'Listen.' Running Tree said.

James listened. 'I can't hear a damned thing.'

'Then you will hear my signal.'

Before either man could move, a shriek shrilled through the night air. The hairs on the back of James's head stood up. Sam. Something was happening to Sam.

As the light began to fail, Burt knew he was in sight of his first hiding hole. The terrain began to get rockier, cactus plants were closer together, denoting an underground water source. The ride had been long and hard and hot. What had kept him going was Sam. Or rather, the thought of what he was going to do with her tonight.

'Soon be there now,' he said matter-of-factly.

'Good. I can't go on much longer.' Sam seemed to sigh the words out.

'Lookin' forward to it, ain't ya,' Burt laughed again. He seemed to spend most of his time laughing, though God knew what about.

'I neither know nor care what you're talking about.' Sam was resigned to the inevitable. She only hoped he'd make some attempt at washing himself first. But she doubted it.

Circling a large sand dune, Burt announced that they had arrived. What Sam saw was a small depression, surrounded on three sides by rocks and small trees, the opening was by way of the sand dune. Under any other circumstances it would have been a welcome sight.

Dismounting, Burt then lifted Sam from her horse, sat her on the sandy ground and proceeded to tie her up again, hands and feet.

'Really, there's no need for this, you know. Where can I go? We're in the middle of nowhere!' Sam tried to reason with Burt, but to no effect. He just kept on tying the rope.

'Got to make sure, missy, don' want you arunnin' off while I get the camp sorted, means I'd have to run after you.'

Having made sure that Sam Was secure, Burt started to gather twigs and grass to make ready a fire. He retrieved an old coffee pot from behind a pile of rocks, along with the coffee beans and dried hog fat he stored there weeks ago.

Emptying the contents of the canteen into the pot, he threw a handful of beans in it and propped it on the twigs and grass. Taking out a match, he lit the cheroot in his mouth, then the fire.

'Gonna be cold, so we'd best keep warm,' he said to Sam.

Burt walked to his horse, removed the saddle and laid it on the ground. Next he took out a bottle of whiskey, half drunk already, and took a mighty swig of it before offering it to Sam.

'No, thank you, I don't drink whiskey.'

'Might loosen you up a bit, missy,' Burt leered at her.

'I doubt that, very much,' Sam replied.

Burt took another long swig out of the bottle and belched. 'Sure does taste fine,' he said.

Standing, he wandered off to the nearest clump of rocks. He came back with four pieces of wood, which he proceeded to hammer into the sand near the already burning fire. Next, he tied a small amount of rope to each stake. Then he moved towards Sam.

What are you going to do?' she asked.

'Oh, jus' make sure you can't run away, is all,' Burt replied.

'I've already told you, there's no point in doing that. I'd die out there.'

'Yeah, well, better safe than sorry,' Burt laughed as he finished tying the ropes. He stood and took another long swig from the bottle, which was almost empty already. Sam saw him approaching unsteadily on his feet.

'Now, what I'm a gonna do, is make

sure you're comfortable, an' in the right position.' He leered at Sam. He kept licking his lips as though he were about to eat a long-awaited meal. Sam was sure that's what he was thinking.

'Please, there's no need to do this,' Sam begged.

'Oh yes there is. It's been a long time, a long time.'

Roughly, he pulled Sam to her feet. Untied the ropes at her ankles, and frog-marched her to the fire. Pushing her down, he grabbed her left ankle and secured it to the stake. He then did the same with her right ankle. Certain that Sam was secure, he untied the ropes that bound her wrists.

Sam went for him then. Managing to score the side of his face with her nails.

'Yeeha! Now that's more like it! I like a woman to put up a fight,' Burt laughed out, then grabbed the wrist of her right hand and tied it to the third stake, moved across and tied her other wrist to the fourth.

Sam was helpless.

He stood for a while, just looking down at her. Sam struggled with the ropes, but to no avail. They were tight, and she didn't have the strength to pull the stakes out of the ground.

Slowly, Burt unbuckled his gunbelt. He let it drop at his feet, certain there was no way she could reach it. Then he removed his trail coat and threw that to the ground, leaning over, he picked up the whiskey bottle and finished it off.

He knelt between Sam's legs and just looked at her. Then he placed both hands on her breasts and leaned on her with all his weight. Sam could see the black, broken stumps of teeth, his green-coloured tongue, the cracked and broken lips approaching and there wasn't a damn thing she could do.

Burt forced his face on hers. She almost gagged at the smell. Not only of his breath, which was fetid, but odour that emanated from the rest of him. Sour smelling. Unclean.

Burt raised himself up on his haunches, the leer on his face had turned into a smirk, he pulled roughly at Sam's skirt, saw the belt, unbuckled it, ripped the skirt off her body. He was visibly drooling now, his eyes had glazed over.

Pulling at her undergarments, he tore them to shreds. He then unbuckled his own belt and pulled his trousers down, he wore no underwear. Sam screamed as his manhood sprang into the cooling night air. She screamed and screamed and screamed.

11

James's first reaction was to run at full speed up the dune. Running Tree managed to stop him with a flying tackle.

'No. This is not the way. We must take care,' Running Tree calmed.

'Yeah, you're right, I guess,' James replied.

'We move off now, but we move off together, each of us know what the other is about to do. Agreed?' Running Tree stared into James's eyes.

'Agreed.'

'Good. Now I circle right, you straight up. Watch for markers. Stay in centre of markers, they point way to camp. You hear my signal, you crawl down dune and get as close as you can to fire,' Running Tree said.

'OK. What are you gonna do?' James asked.

'I kill Burt.'

It was said with no malice, no hatred.

Just a bare matter-of-fact statement. James knew he would kill Burt. Trouble was, James really didn't want to stay around and watch.

'We ready?' Running Tree said.

'You bet.' James replied.

Together they rose and went their separate ways.

★ ★ ★

Seth began rooting through the wagon. Some food, some weapons and ammunition, but not much else. He was hoping for greater things. Gold, maybe. Cash. The gang had obviously been robbers, so where did they stash their loot?

Then he found the whiskey bottle. Brand new and unopened.

'Jacob,' he called. 'Seems like we can have a little drink. What d'you say?' Seth held the bottle up. The bullet smashed through the glass, showering him with whiskey.

Seth fell to the floor. Uninjured, he wanted to stay that way.

'Seth,' Jacob called. You OK?'

'Yeah. More'n I can say for the whiskey, Goddamnit!'

'Where's the shot come from?'

'I don't know. I was ready to wet ma whistle, didn't notice.'

'Can you see Lewis?' Jacob asked.

'Nope,' Seth replied. 'But he musta heard the shot.'

'Stay low, keep your eyes peeled,' Jacob said as he pulled out his own Colt.

'Well I sure as hell ain't gonna start dancin',' Seth shouted back at him.

Jacob crawled across to the rocks on his left. Raising his head, he tried to see if he could catch a glimpse of Lewis. Before he had time to take a good look, another shot rang out, ricocheting off the rock, sending a shower of granite dust into his eyes.

'Goddamn it to hell,' he muttered.

'You OK, Jacob?' Seth shouted.

'Will you to hell keep your damn voice quiet!' Jacob exploded.

'You're OK, then,' Seth whispered.

This time, Seth had been able to see in

the semi-darkness the muzzle flash. He knew where the sniper was. He coughed loudly.

Jacob raised his head slightly and looked in Seth's direction. Seth, without saying a word, pointed to Jacob's right. Jacob nodded.

The two men began a long and slow crawl. There was still no sign of Lewis. And who in the hell was it that was taking potshots at them?

They were circling around to get one on each side of their adversary when a third shot rang out, narrowly missing Seth.

'Before you ask, I'm all right,' Seth whispered. 'Jus' keep me covered.'

With that, Seth raised himself to his feet and crouching, made for the rocks on his left. Jacob kept up a volley of shots.

The gunman kept his head down. When their camp had been attacked the night before, he had been taking a crap. He'd heard the noise all right, but there was no way he was coming back to help out.

He'd laid low.

All through the day, he'd kept a quiet watch on the camp. He'd watched as the funeral was held for the Indian. Saw the rocks being bundled on to the dead bodies of his *compadres*. He waited.

When two of the party left the camp, he knew that cut the odds down from 5-1 to 3-1. Still against, but more acceptable.

Waiting for nightfall, after all day in the sun with relatively little shade and no water, he decided to make his move. Slugging the boy had been child's play. Damn fools to let a kid like that keep watch anyway.

He now knew there was just the two old-timers in the camp. He could handle them easily.

Taking careful aim, he'd shot at Seth. Missed.

Then he shot at Jacob. Missed.

Must be getting old, he thought, *else this gun's no good.*

But he was still sure he could handle the old men. He was sure right up until the bullet entered his left eye and blew the back of his head out.

★ ★ ★

Seth stood over the body. He'd killed before, but not for a long, long time, and always in self-defence. The sight of this man's head exposed to the elements made even his stomach churn.

Seth recognized this was one of Burt's men. Somehow, he didn't get shot the previous night. Jacob stood beside Seth.

'Never thought you could hit the high side of a barn at your age, let alone kill someone,' Jacob chuckled.

'Yeah, well . . . ' Seth had no need to finish the sentence.

'Pity 'bout the whiskey, though, Jacob smacked his lips. 'Been a long time since I tasted whiskey.'

'I'm goin' for a leak. Where in the hell's that damn boy got to. He musta heard the shootin'.

'I'll scout aroun',' he can't be far off, Jacob said.

173

Seth wandered out into the prairie and, undoing his fly-button, sent a hot stream of liquid into the nearest tumble-weed.

'Jesus H. Christ,' Seth spluttered.

Lying face up under the tumbleweed was Lewis.

'I jus' done piss all over you, boy. What in the hell you a lying there for?'

'I woulda thought that was obvious, even to you,' Lewis stood, hands tied behind his back. 'I got drygulched, didn't even see 'im.'

'Turn around, boy, I'll loosen them ropes,' Seth said.

'Now I'm covered in piss. Goddamnit.' Lewis started to brush off the caked-on and moist sand.

'This here's leaking country, boy. You jus' remember that.' Seth laughed all the way back to the campsite.

'You found him then,' Jacob asked.

'Sure did. Me an' ma pecker, we found him all right,' Seth answered and laughed his boots off.

James reached the top of the sand dune and laid up there waiting for Running Tree's signal. The night air was cold. There was a steady breeze. He absent-mindedly watched the tiny grains of sand gently moving in the wind.

Then he heard a cooing sound. That must be it, he thought. At least, I hope to hell it is.

With that, he started to crawl down the far side of the sand dune towards Burt's camp. Towards Sam.

Running Tree was now right behind Burt. Knife at the ready. He hoped that Sam didn't give the game away.

She didn't. She caught a glimpse of Running Tree and directed her attention towards Burt.

'My, that's the biggest one I've ever seen,' she said.

'Goddamn, it is big ain't it,' Burt looked down at himself. A grin was on his face like that of a small kid being given candy.

He then looked back at Sam and said, 'You ain't joshin' me are you? I know 'bout you women.'

'No, honest. It is big,' Sam smiled. At least, her lips smiled. Any man who had an inkling of sensitivity about him would have seen her eyes. They didn't smile.

'Lot o' women said that. Never seen nobody else's, so how'm I supposed to know? Sure looks big to me, though.' he grinned, for him, sheepishly.

'Now we'll jus' find out how it fits,' he said and he started to lean in closer.

Sam still smiled.

The butt of the knife caught Burt on the side of the head. Running Tree pushed him over on to his back and stood astride him. Burt was out cold.

In one swift movement, Running Tree brought the blade down on to Burt's right ear. Blood spurted everywhere. Burt came to.

He didn't feel the pain at first, he felt a warmth on his face and it took him a few seconds to realize that, instead of being sated, something else had happened.

Slowly he raised his hand to his right ear. He felt nothing. Nothing was there but warm stickiness.

The scream, when it came, shook James to the core. He ran into the campsite, rifle cocked and ready to find Burt on the ground rolling around in agony.

He felt relief when he saw Running Tree was all right. Then delight when he saw Sam.

James knelt by her side and held her face in his hands. Even with sun-cracked lips and her hair and face covered in sand and dirt, she was still the most beautiful woman he had ever seen.

'Oh, James, it's good to see you. And you, Running Tree. But I fear you have me somewhat disadvantaged.'

James sat up, she was spreadeagled on the ground, still attached to the stakes. James started to look down her body. When he saw that she was almost fully exposed, he was glad of the darkness. It hid the fact that his face went a bright crimson.

'Oh, yeah — uh — sorry — um — where's

the knife?' He hurriedly wrapped her torn skirt round her middle. Running Tree told him, 'Untie ropes.'

James was all fingers and thumbs but eventually he had Sam free.

'He didn't — you know — er — did he?' James asked.

'No, don't worry James, he didn't get time to do anything. Although another minute or so and . . . ' she left the sentence unfinished.

'Now he never will,' Running Tree said, and, when they looked around, they both saw what it was he held in his hand.

'Oh, my God,' James spluttered.

Sam looked away.

'Take Sam to our horses and wait for me there,' Running Tree said.

James and Sam knew better than to argue. Helping her stand, James couldn't resist a little hug. 'It's sure good to see you again, Sam,' he said. 'I thought I'd never see your pretty face again.'

Sam smiled demurely as he led her off to the top of the sand dune, back to their horses.

Burt was not rolling around so much by now. The pain, although not subsiding any, had been replaced by fear. He had vaguely watched James and Sam walk off. He now turned his attention to the Indian. He recognized the man. He'd seen him before. Sure, he'd been with them other two Indians, he'd been next to one he'd shot.

Running Tree just stared at the prostrate man.

'Come on, now, you ain't gonna kill me, are you? Burt pleaded. 'I mean, look what you done, boy, look what you done. I ain't even got an ear no more.'

Running Tree still didn't say anything, in his mind's eye he could see Moonface and Wolf Wind. He wasn't sure that this man had been the one who killed Wolf Wind, but he'd watched as he'd killed his other brother. Now he must pay.

Silently, he grabbed Burt's legs and tied them to the stakes Burt had sunk. Pulling at his arms, he then tied both hands. Burt was now staked out on the very bed of pleasure he had prepared.

The pain in his head was excruciating, blood still pumped, although slower now as the veins had relaxed a little. But being spreadeagled, his legs wide apart, he felt like he'd been ripped in two.

Running Tree began to chant, quietly, almost to himself.

'What you plannin' on doin', you heathen bastard?' Burt had never been more scared in his mean, ugly life.

Running Tree continued his chant.

'Think you're scaring me, don't you. Well I ain't see. You don' scare me none,' Burt shouted.

Running Tree almost smiled. But not quite. He pulled out his knife and ran his thumb along the edge. Burt screamed at him, but Running Tree didn't hear him. Approaching Burt, he knelt down on his chest and lifted his head by his hair.

'What you doin', you wouldn' kill a defenceless man, now would you? I challenge you. Yeah, that's what you like, isn't it, a challenge to the death? Fight me man to man, if'n you can. That's what you people do, isn't it?' Burt was almost sobbing.

Running Tree slowly, deliberately brought the blade of the knife to Burt's scalp. Although he'd only practised scalping on wild animals, he knew what to do. Burt could see that. The blade went into the scalp at the forehead, Running Tree pulled at the hair, the skin came off easily exposing the white skull beneath. Burt screamed, but Running Tree cut on.

Burt could hear, rather than feel, the skin leave his head. It sounded like a man pulling his boot out of a mud puddle. A soft sucking sound. Then he blacked out.

★　★　★

James tore off a part of his shirt and doused it in water from the canteen. Gently, he began patting Sam's face. The sand and dirt came off easily enough, but the horror in her eyes stayed there. He wanted to hold her. Tell her everything was gonna be all right. But he'd never been with a woman before. Never had either the opportunity or seen one he'd like to get to know.

Sure, he'd been tempted, when they'd been riding the range looking for adventure, and finding none. Heading for the nearest town, they'd all walked past the bordellos, each of them making excuses why they weren't going in. But the thought of paying a woman for sex didn't appeal to James. He hoped that one day he'd meet the woman of his dreams. Now he knew he had. But the look in her eyes would take a lot of loving to get rid of.

'There, you're back to your beautiful self again,' he said gently.

'Thank you, James, I even feel better — now.' She closed her eyes, as if in sleep.

'Can I get you anythin', coffee, water, a blanket?' he asked.

'A blanket please, I feel really tired, all of a sudden.' She closed her eyes again.

James went to the horses and got his blanket. He was sure she was asleep when he returned. Gently, he laid the blanket over her, tucking the edges underneath her so the wind wouldn't get in.

'I think I love you,' he whispered and, very gently, he kissed her on the cheek and then the lips.

Sam's eyes opened. Fear and terror filled her face. Then she saw James.

'I'm sorry, I'm truly sorry, it's just that — ,' he stopped, helpless.

'It's OK, James. I heard what you said.' She put her arms around his neck and pulled him to her.

They stayed that way until the rhythmic rise and fall of her chest told James that she was finally asleep.

He eased her arms from his neck, tucked them under the blanket and kissed her forehead. She smiled in her sleep.

If James could have whooped for joy right then and there, he would. But he was frightened of wakening her again. He walked away a few paces, balled his fists and whispered, 'Yes!'

★ ★ ★

Burt came to in hell. He was sure of that. Red blurred his vision. Pain coursed through his body the way whiskey hit his gut. He opened his mouth to scream again, but saw Running Tree sitting quietly beside him.

He closed his eyes. He knew he was going to die. He just didn't know how long it would take.

His shirt had been removed, looking down he saw his own ears lying on his chest. Then he screamed.

Running Tree did not stir. He seemed to be asleep, except that his eyes were open. He sat cross-legged to the left of Burt, hunting knife in his lap.

'How long's this gonna last,' he sobbed.

'Long enough,' came the reply.

'Jus' finish me off, I ain't beggin' for mercy. Jus' finish me off.' Burt felt the salt tears course down his cheeks.

Running Tree also noted them. These white men were not human beings. The tracks of the tears had cut through some of the grime that embedded Burt's face, leaving a relatively clean trail behind them. Running Tree was disgusted.

'Jus' cos I killed one o' your tribe, I mean, that's what it's all about, ain't it? We're at war, you an' me,' Burt coughed, his ear moved to one side of his heaving chest. 'An' get those damn things off me.'

'Me thought you'd like to have them nearby,' Running Tree said.

'Well 'me' thought wrong. Get them off.' Burt tried to move his body to shake them off, but the fire in his head stopped any movement.

'White man talk too much.' Running Tree stood, knife in hand. He brought the hilt of the knife down on Burt's mouth, breaking teeth and splitting his lips, then he reached into Burt's mouth and cut his tongue out. He placed this between his ears.

Burt blacked out again. Running Tree sat down again.

Running Tree could wait.

★ ★ ★

Sam awoke with a start. She started to struggle, thinking the blanket had her pegged out on the stakes again. She saw James, sitting right beside her, and she lay still. He smiled warmly at her. 'Here, fresh coffee. Just brewed it myself.' He handed her a mug of the steaming, black liquid.

She sipped at it gratefully, only now realising how dry her throat was. James stood and retrieved the stick from Running Tree's blanket, plunged it into the sand behind Sam's head and with the other blanket laid it over the stick forming a tent, just as Running Tree had taught him, to protect Sam's face from the blazing sun.

Sam felt groggy. Too much sleep, she guessed. But the height of the sun meant it was way past 11 o'clock. Then the memory of yesterday's forced journey, and of the horror of last night flooded back into her mind. A frown creased her brow.

James leant forward and brushed the frown aside. 'It's OK, now,' he said.

'Nothing's ever gonna harm you again, not while I'm around, and I plan to be around a long time.'

Sam smiled. She knew that he had been attracted to her on that very first day. When was that now, one, two, three days ago? She couldn't remember. She could remember imagining what he might look like without the beard he was wearing. Suddenly, she sat up, knocking the tent-blanket off the stick. 'Your beard! You shaved off your beard!'

'Well, I figured it was time,' he said sheepishly. Once again he blushed deeply. This time Sam saw it and smiled.

'Beards are useful things,' he said. 'Keep you warm in the winter, sun off your face in the summer, but when it comes to kissing a beautiful woman, hell, it ain't no use at all.'

Again Sam smiled as James leaned forward and kissed her cheek.

★ ★ ★

Running Tree waited patiently. He neither hated nor enjoyed what he was doing. It just had to be done. The spirit, if indeed this white man had a spirit, must not be allowed to remain whole. Before he died it must be separated.

Burt came to again. He was choking on his own blood. He opened his mouth, 'Aaagghhhhh!' was all he could manage. Then he remembered his tongue. Lowering his eyes, he already knew what would be resting on his bare chest. Sure enough, there were three objects there now. Trouble was, he had great difficulty in deciding which was what. Burt actually laughed. A hoarse, gargled, gagged laugh.

'It is good you still can laugh,' Running Tree said. 'For your life is almost at its close. Let me tell you who you killed. The Indian, the member of my tribe, was my brother. In the shooting of two days ago, my other brother was also killed, I am not sure if you are guilty of that, but if it was one of your gang, they are all dead. You are not — yet.'

Burt closed his eyes, the pain in his mouth and his head kept washing over him in waves. Several times while Running Tree was talking to him he'd almost blacked out. He'd even forgotten about his scalp.

Running Tree sat and stared at the bloody mess before him. He felt no pity, no regret, certainly no remorse. One more object needed to be removed from the man's body, then he would be free. Free to roam the world of his own hell.

★ ★ ★

Sam was feeling stronger now. Mentally and physically. James went over what had happened at the campsite that night. She was shocked to hear of Hank and Brad, but pleased that Seth, Jacob and Lewis were still alive and well and waiting for them with the aeroplane.

She told him of her own fears for his life. How that when she had been dragged from beneath the wagon by Burt, she was certain that he was dead.

What she didn't tell him then, but would later, was how much she hoped he was alive.

The screams from the other side of the sand dune brought all her fears to the surface. James held her. The passion they both felt was inexplicable. Sam had never felt this way before. James certainly hadn't. They savoured the moment.

This was not the time nor the place. But that time and place would come, they both knew that.

Gently, James laid Sam back down on the ground, covered her with the blanket and rigged the tent. She protested, but he assured her that the blanket, rather than keeping her warm, would actually help to keep her cooler. Besides, he had said to her, she must get as much rest as possible for the journey back to the campsite. It would take at least another day, and possibly night.

She knew he was right. She closed her eyes, and, even after all the sleep she had had, within minutes she slept again.

James sat and watched over her. Ever

since he could remember he didn't know what it was he wanted out of life. He thought adventure, but that had proved disastrous. His closest friends were now dead. But as soon as he saw Sam, he knew. He lay back in the sand, put his hands behind his head and smiled. Waiting for Running Tree.

★ ★ ★

Burt was delirious. The sun beating down on his exposed skull had started to overheat his brain, literally. The protection of hair and skin and blood vessels had been removed. He was frying. Nevertheless, his eyes flickered open, he blinked, saw Running Tree and he groaned. He was still alive!

'Aaaggghhhh!'

Running Tree leaned over the inert form, knife in his hand. Now he was ready for the final act. Not death, that would come later. Maybe the buzzards. Maybe the sun. Carefully, Running Tree slipped the knife under Burt's nose and sliced it off.

'Aaaaaggggghhhhhhl'

Running Tree stood up, wiped the bloody knife on his breeches and sheathed it.

The man who was once Burt stared blindly into the sun. He would get no rest until his death arrived. And now, he would see it coming.

Running Tree turned, and without a word, left the man in the blazing sun.

'Aaaaaaggggggggghhhhhhhhh!'

Running Tree did not turn.

* * *

'It is done,' he told James and Sam, 'Now we return.'

Running Tree had brought a horse for Sam, and James helped her into the saddle. He insisted she wear the blanket over her head, and gratefully she accepted.

James had a million questions he wanted to ask Running Tree. But he didn't ask one.

They began their long, hot journey
back to the campsite.

12

Seth and Jacob, with a little help from Lewis, buried the final, they hoped, body of Burt's gang. Even digging a shallow grave, in this heat, took it out of them.

Seth mopped his brow. 'Think I'll take another nap before we cover this saddle-bum with rocks,' he said. 'This heat's sure getting to me.'

'Mus' be 100 degrees out here,' Lewis said. The hat he was wearing was soaked with sweat, even though he tried to dry it off every few minutes.

'What I wouldn't give for a nice long, cool, beer,' Jacob fantasised.

'I'd even take a cold bath,' Seth replied.

'Jesus H, Seth, that'd really be pushing the boat out!' Jacob laughed.

'I ain't never seen no boat,' Lewis said.

Both men stopped their laughter and looked at Lewis.

'What the hell's that got to do with anythin'?' Seth asked.

'Nuthin'. Just thought I'd mention it, is all. Ain't never seen no sea, either. Sure would be nice to just jump in it though, wouldn't it?'

Seth looked at Jacob and both looked towards the heavens.

'I'll be under the wagon, if'n you need me,' Seth said, and wandered off to grab a nap.

'Guess I'll join you, Seth, now there ain't no snakes there.' Jacob followed.

Lewis sat by the fire, poured himself another coffee, took a mouthful, then spat it out. 'Hell, it's too danged hot for that!' he said to himself.

Moving away from the fire, he settled under the shade of a small clump of rocks, pulled his hat over his eyes, and dreamed.

★ ★ ★

Seth was not sure what had woken him, but instantly he was alert. Something was not quite right. He elbowed Jacob.

'What the hell—' Jacob began.

'Shhhh. I don't know what it is, but there's something out there.' Seth slowly moved behind one of the wagon's wheels. Jacob moved across behind another. They could both see Lewis, fast asleep with his mouth wide open, making enough noise to wake the dead.

Seth and Jacob drew their weapons. Seth had to check his as it was an old Navy Colt he'd removed from the body they'd just buried. Checking the chamber, he found the gun was empty. Slowly, he had moved to his gunbelt and, one by one, he loaded the gun. The noise each bullet made as it slid into the chamber was, to him, deafening.

Jacob watched Seth. He was sure the old fool would shoot his foot off one day. Although Seth had had, and used, a sidearm all his life, he never quite got the hang of them. Jacob breathed out a sigh of relief as Seth finished loading the gun, closed the chamber and cocked the hammer.

'You make sure you don't shoot somebody you know,' Jacob whispered.

'Remember I'm to your right, an' Lewis is over yonder.'

'That meant to be funny?' Seth scowled.

'No. That's meant to let you know where I am,' Jacob replied, a wry grin on his face.

'Shoulda shot you years ago,' Seth mumbled. 'Put me outta my misery.'

'You'da starved to death by now, way you cook,' Jacob said.

'Least I wouldn't have to force your grub down my face,' Seth retorted.

'Well, you're still here, ain't you—'

Jacob's reply was cut short by the arrow that hit the side of the wagon.

'Where'n the hell did that come from?' Seth said.

'Beats me,' Jacob replied.

A second arrow hit the wooden hub of the wheel right in front of Seth's face. 'Shit!' Seth began to edge backwards, Jacob followed.

Their progress was halted by the feel of cold steel in their necks. Both men froze. Slowly they turned their heads and saw the Indians.

Lewis, snoring like a banshee, awoke to see a tomahawk inches from his nose.

'What!' was all he managed to get out before the stone head of the tomahawk knocked him unconscious.

Seth and Jacob were both trussed up like a turkey and dragged to the middle of the campsite. Stakes were banged into the ground and all three men tied to the stakes.

Out of the bright sun a giant shadow stepped. To Jacob, the figure was black against the light. The giant figure walked along and looked at each man in turn before turning away.

Seth could make out at least eight Indians. He hadn't seen so many in years. All were covered in warpaint, as were their horses.

'Where in the hell did they spring from. There ain't been no Indians roun' here in two, three years,' Seth whispered.

'Well there sure as hell are now,' Jacob replied. 'They seem to be takin' an unusual interest in ol' Wolf Wind, yonder.'

Seth craned his neck and looked towards the final resting place of Wolf Wind. The Indians had formed a circle and seemed to be chanting the way Running Tree had.

'Seems we got a case of mistaken identity, here,' Jacob said. 'I reckon those critters think we done it.'

'Are they goin' to kill us?' Lewis asked.

'Not if we can help it,' Jacob said. And he called out to the group of Indians.

His voice seemed to ignite some flame in the Indians. As one, they all started to holler and yell and whoop as only Indians can, and then ran towards the three prostrate men. Seth and Jacob and Lewis all saw their raised tomahawks and spears and bows loaded with arrows.

Lewis peed his pants, Seth and Jacob gulped.

* * *

Burt went through the motions of opening his eyes. He'd been unconscious, but he didn't know for how long. His eyes were dry, the sun burning into them, he could hardly move them.

He moved his head to look at the stakes that bound his hands. The pain that shot down his neck almost blacked him out again.

Slowly, he remembered what had happened. 'Aaaggghhhh!' he shouted. But there was no one to hear him scream.

He struggled frantically, kicking out with his legs and trying to pull him arms out of the ropes. The pain was so intense he began to black out again. He stopped moving. Took deep breaths. Sweat rolled from his severed forehead, mixed with fresh blood, and rolled into his unprotected eyes. At least that moistened them.

Turning his head carefully to one side in an effort to dislodge the excess sweat from his eyes, he felt, rather than saw, a shadow.

He kept still, trying to focus. He heard a gentle plop to his left. He turned his head and saw the first buzzard arrive.

'Aaaggghhhh!'

in the blanket had placed over her head so she wouldn't burn. From where he

★ ★ ★

Running Tree had been silent. He rode ahead of James and Sam, not seeming to be bothered by the heat and the dust. He sat erect on his pony, his long legs hanging limply. James noted the moccasins on his feet, the delicate embroidery and coloured beads, sewn on lovingly by someone on the soft deer skin.

James's impression of Indians had been like most white folks who'd never seen or met them. Hostile, savage heathens. People who'd as soon kill you as look at you. Yet James realized this was not true. Running Tree and his two brothers spoke English. They'd helped. In fact, James knew that if it hadn't been for Running Tree, not only would he be dead, but so would Sam.

For that reason alone, James had nothing but admiration for the man.

He looked across at Sam, A warm feeling filled him to his boots. He'd never met a woman like her before. So strong and brave and beautiful. She was draped in the blanket he'd placed over her head so she wouldn't burn. From where he sat, she almost looked like a squaw.

Running Tree stopped his pony and looked skywards. Shielding his eyes, James looked up. In the distance he could just pick out three or four dark specks. Birds he supposed.

Sam looked skywards, she knew what the birds were and where they were going. She cast a glance at Running Tree, but his face was expressionless. The dark brown eyes, high cheek bones, the light brown skin, the slightly hooked nose, Sam took all this in. She too had never met an Indian. The muscles in his arms and legs though, told a different story. They were tensed. She thought she knew what he was feeling. She thought she felt the same way.

Running Tree kicked his pony on. He didn't say a word. He didn't have to.

* * *

One by one, more buzzards landed. Fighting amongst themselves and making a raucous cacophony that was driving Burt mad.

He knew what a chicken-shit breed buzzards were. They had no guts. He despised them. One by one they approached his body to within a few feet, just checking, before flapping their wings and backing off, landing back on the ground ten or twelve feet away and fighting with one of their kind again.

Burt's senses had risen above his pain. He could hear the whoosh as their wings flapped, hear their beaks close with a clack. He knew that pretty soon, those very same beaks would reduce him to a skeleton.

Philosophically, for Burt, he even began to wonder how long it would take. Would they gorge themselves on his body if he blacked out again, only to retreat when his screams drove them off. Would he feel those sharpened instruments of destruction bite and rip his flesh off his bones. He grinned. A maniacal grin. He felt a prod on his bare skull, shook his head, 'Aaagggghhhhh!' Wings flapped and retreated.

Not long now. He thought.

* * *

'Whoa!' Jacob shouted at the top of his voice. His shout stopped the Indians in their tracks. 'English? Do you un'erstan' English?' he pleaded.

'Moonface and Wolf Wind have been killed. Not by us. By the rest of the bodies over yonder, under them rocks.

'Running Tree is out hunting down their leader right this minute. He'll be back soon.' Jacob kept his head up, out-staring the Indians.

Seth added under his breath, 'At least we hope to Christ he is!'

The Indians stood where they had stopped. They discussed this piece of information amongst themselves. The giant man moved forward. Seth could see he wasn't afraid. He could also see that the man had a loathing in his eyes for all white men. A contempt that might cloud his judgement.

'White man lie,' he said and raised his spear.

'Now why'n the hell would we do that?' Jacob responded.

This seemed to throw the giant man for a while as he couldn't think of a reason.

'Why don't we jus' wait here,' Seth added, 'Running Tree will come back. He's a good man.'

The Indians talked again. An agreement was reached.

'We wait,' the giant man said and sat cross-legged in front of the three men.

'Well, d' you think we could wait under the wagon?' Seth asked.

'Ain't as if we could escape or nothin',' Jacob said.

The giant Indian thought about this.

'I mean, if'n we're right an' Running Tree comes back, he's gonna be awful sore you got his friends staked out like a buffalo hide.' Jacob was convincing.

The giant man stepped forward and

cut the bonds that held them. They were still covered by the spears and tomahawks. The Indians led the three men over to the wagon and tied them, loosely, to the wheels.

Although Seth and Jacob noticed that in turn each of the Indians had looked at the strange object on the wagon, not one of them had asked any questions.

The giant walked across the campsite and squatted opposite Jacob.

'Tell, what happened here,' he said.

Jacob described the meeting between themselves, James and his boys, the Indians and then Burt's gang.

The giant Indian listened intently without offering any comment. When Jacob had finished he just got up and walked off to inform the other Indians.

★ ★ ★

'Aaagghhhh!'

Burt knew he was fighting a losing battle. The buzzards were getting closer, their fighting more frenzied, the smell of death filled their senses and they were becoming impatient.

One bird swooped forward and landed on Burt's chest. The force took the breath out of Burt. He was too weak to move enough to shake the bird loose. The buzzard's eyes peered into his. It was as if he was willing the man to die.

The beak swooped down. The tongue, then one of the ears disappeared.

'Aaaggghhhhh!'

The buzzard flew back to the pack.

Immediately a fight broke out that sent feathers flying in all directions. The birds seemed to forget all about Burt. So intense was the squabbling that two of the buzzards, who were pecking at each other so fiercely they were drawing blood, finished up between Burt's legs. A flurry of feathers and talons, beaks clashing. 'Aaaggghhhh!'

★ ★ ★

Running Tree halted his pony and dismounted. They were back on the

207

perimeter of the desert. That strange place where two environments met. The desert, yellow and blindingly hot. The beginnings of the prairie, still very sandy but inexplicably green, locked together in a battle that would take a thousand years to resolve.

James helped Sam from the saddle. The blanket had kept the sun from her neck, and already she was feeling stronger, still tired and weary from her ordeal, but decidedly stronger. James's arms encircled her for longer than was absolutely necessary, a fact that was not missed by Running Tree, who actually grinned.

'We camp here for night, tomorrow, three hours, we make campsite.' Running Tree busied himself soothing his pony.

James released Sam and helped her sit on the blanket. Once she was settled, he scouted around and found enough twigs and dried grass to act as kindling. Coffee would not be long.

Running Tree unsaddled Sam's mount

and placed the leather saddle behind her so she could rest on it. James lit the fire, using his last match.

'Oh, how I long for a bath,' Sam said, stretching her legs and easing the stiffness of the saddle from her joints. 'I've never ridden for so long without a break.'

'You sure can ride well,' James said.

'I had enough practice. I've been riding since before I can remember. But usually around the park in Boston. The weather is a little more forgiving than here,' Sam smiled at James.

He melted and had to avert his eyes as he felt the hot flush creeping up his face.

'What do you intend to do, when we get back?' James's question was tentative.

'I don't know. I hope the aeroplane is still in one piece. The idea was to learn to fly properly in a place where I could do the least damage. Seems where I picked caused more damage than I ever imagined.'

'I guess Burt's gang were just looking for trouble anyway,' James said. 'If it hadn't been us, it would've been somebody else.'

'That's me all right. Always in the wrong place at the wrong time.' Sam sighed.

'Oh, I wouldn't say that. If you hadn't been in the right place at the right time, I'd never had met you.' James was still blushing.

'Coffee ready.' Running Tree poured out two cups, he handed one to Sam, the other to James.

'Aren't you having any?' Sam asked.

'One of the white man's drinks I haven't quite got the taste for, yet,' he said with a wry smile.

Darkness began to fall. The air was getting cooler, a blessed relief to the heat of the day. Sam and James watched the sun go down. For James, who had watched it go down many times before, it was the most beautiful sight he had ever seen. He wondered why he hadn't noticed it before.

Running Tree was looking back in the direction in which they had travelled.

He'd seen no more buzzards. He wondered how long Burt would last. Long, he hoped, but there was no feeling in the thought. Just the inevitability of death.

Running Tree knew that Burt was still alive. The buzzards hadn't taken to the air again. He knew they were waiting for Burt to die, as was he.

James tucked Sam up into the blanket, stoked the fire, and sat watching her until her steady breathing told him she was asleep.

Running Tree turned to James. 'You love this woman.'

It was not a question, it was a statement of fact.

'Yeah. I guess I do,' James replied.

'She is special. I can see that,' Running Tree said, and without further comment he turned on his side and slept.

The night was uneventful. Sam was the first to awaken. Quietly she stirred the dying embers of the fire, gathered some dry grass, and within a matter of minutes, the fire was blazing hot enough to put the coffee pot back on.

James woke up to the smell of fresh coffee wafting up his nose. His eyes were filled with the smiling face of Sam as she held the cup out to him.

'Thank you kindly, ma'am,' he said formally taking the cup.

'Well I declare,' Sam said with a Southern drawl. 'Ah do believe you are welcome, sah.'

They both laughed and Running Tree sat up. 'Water?' Sam asked.

'Time I tried coffee again, I think,' Running Tree said. Sam poured him a small mugful. Running Tree sipped it, then spat it out. 'I have water, I think. Not ready for coffee.'

Sam and James laughed, but with, rather than at, Running Tree.

James saddled the two horses, lifted Sam into the saddle, and before the sun had time to start cooking them again, they resumed their journey.

★　★　★

The campsite had been quiet during the night. The Indians had kept the fire going, and, every hour or so, came across to check that their prisoners were still there. Jacob had no doubt that, as long as he were successful, Running Tree would return that morning. He knew the Indian would have no trouble tracking Burt and Sam. He just hoped that Running Tree had come out the victor.

Seth, on the other hand, wasn't so sure about Running Tree. Although Jacob had virtually staked their lives on his return, with Seth's agreement, he still wasn't sure. Running Tree was a young, frustrated brave. Probably never fought in an Indian war in his life, Burt on the other hand was as devious as they came. He knew every trick in the book.

Lewis had no doubts whatsoever. The innocence and trust of youth completely obliterated every other thought. He was positive Running Tree, Sam and James would return unscathed. Already, he was scanning as much of the horizon as the rope allowed, to catch first sight of them.

The sun began its lazy crawl into the sky, brushing the darkness away the way a woman brushes the kitchen floor of dirt. Soon the heat would be there too, still they were sheltered. Seth just hoped he was still alive come sundown.

* * *

Burt was in shock. The night had been one long nightmare after another. The buzzards were still there, craven cowards that they were. He had drifted in and out of consciousness all night. If the buzzards didn't wake him with their screeching or tentative pecking, then the insects sure did.

There was little he could do about the tickling sensation followed by the small nips and bites in his groin. But when the pesky things started crawling over his face and tried to burrow down the cracks in his lips, or where his hair line used to be, that's what make him shake his head violently, trying to throw them off.

He was weak. He knew that. How he

had survived the night was a mystery to him. He was never sure if he was dreaming, or actually seeing the stars from his lidless eyes. He never quite knew the difference between being asleep and being awake. All he wanted now was to die. As quickly as possible.

He sighed deeply. Even the air he exhaled hurt his swollen stump of a tongue. He couldn't lick his lips. Tears fell from his eyes and he turned his head to allow them to fall down his cheeks. He stared straight into the upturned sting of a scorpion.

The scorpion struck. Twice. The second time hit him in the eyeball. He didn't move. He didn't even shout. He smiled.

It wouldn't be long now. He could feel the paralysis slowly moving over his body. It sure hurt like hell. But he didn't care. He'd wondered what a scorpion sting felt like, and still he didn't know. He never would.

The circle of buzzards tightened. They knew he was in the death throes. They had no need to wait now. One by one they ripped and tore at Burt. And he saw them do it.

* * *

Running Tree saw the smoke first. The campsite was only another hour away. Strange though, he thought, no one was keeping a lookout. Even at this distance, someone would have noticed their imminent arrival.

Maybe he was being too cautious. But he'd grown up fast since escaping from the Reservation. Running Tree decided to follow his instincts. Instead of riding straight into the camp, he began a detour, bringing them in from the side behind the wagon.

James noticed first, the smoke, then the change of direction.

'Something wrong?' he asked.

'Not sure,' Running Tree replied evasively.

'We've changed direction,' James said. What's wrong?'

'Probably nothing. But no one has signalled that they have seen us. Strange.'

'Maybe they're still asleep,' James suggested.

'No, fire has been stoked, saw rising embers. Much smoke. Someone is up and about.'

'What do you suggest, then?' Sam asked.

'We circle west, come in behind wagon. I go first, make sure all well. I signal you follow. I no signal, you no follow.'

'We've come too far for that, Running Tree, we're in this together.' James held his hand out to Running Tree. It was the first obvious sign of friendship between the two men.

'As you wish.' Running Tree gripped James's wrist, James gripped his.

'But Sam waits. She no go in with us. Agreed?' Running Tree added.

'Absolutely,' James smiled and they released their grip.

It took them an hour and a half sweeping round to the west before they could see into the campsite clearly. It looked deserted. There was no sign of Seth or Jacob or Lewis. Yet the fire burned brightly.

Running Tree reined his pony to a halt and dismounted. Motioned to the other two to do the same. They were only two hundred yards from the campsite, and still no greeting.

Sam held on to the three horses as James and Running Tree crept forwards. James following his companion's imprints in the sand.

As they neared the wagon, they could plainly see Lewis. He was tied to the wagon wheel as he had been all night.

Running Tree halted and pointed so that James could also see. Without a word Running Tree slithered forward and rounded Lewis, cutting him free in one swift move.

Lewis shouted in surprise, more than anything else.

'Good to see you back, son.' It was Seth who spoke. He'd never doubt this man again.

'Where's James and Sam?' Seth asked. Running Tree put his fingers to his lips and pointed to the rear.

'Good to see you, Running Tree,' Jacob added. 'Real good.'

'Seems like some o' your friends from the Reservation came out looking for you. Thought we killed Moonface and Wolf Wind.' Seth motioned to the other side of the camp.

The giant Indian was standing completely alone. Running Tree's face broke out into the biggest grin Seth and Jacob had ever seen.

With a loud whoop, Running Tree bounded across the campsite straight towards the giant.

'It is good to see you, my friend,' the giant said.

Running Tree was on one knee. 'I am honoured that you sought to help me and my brothers,' Running Tree said.

The two men lapsed into their native tongue, neither Seth nor Jacob, and certainly not Lewis, despite his schooling, could understand a single word they said.

Soon the giant Indian walked across

the campsite to the wagon and held up his right hand, palm forwards. 'I thank you for your help. I am sorry to have doubted your word. Peace.'

With that, as if by magic, the rest of the Indians arrived on horseback bringing the giant's horse with them. With a single wave and a collective whoop, they rode off.

'What in blazes was that all about?' asked Seth.

'I tell them of our misfortunes. How we all help one another. Persuade them to return to Reservation. They all have wives and children. They must be cared for. Their anger at the deaths of my brothers was eased by my vengeance. They go in peace.'

James disappeared and brought Sam into the campsite. He tethered the horse while Sam gave first Seth, then Jacob then Lewis a firm hug in greeting.

'You OK, missy?' Seth asked.

'I'm fine now, Seth. Seeing you all alive and well,' she answered.

'Well it's damn cheered us up seein' as

how you all are back in one piece,' Jacob said.

'An' Burt?' Seth asked.

'There is now no Burt,' was all Running Tree answered. For the sake of Sam, no one asked any more questions.

'Let's get some coffee,' Seth said.

'I not think I try again,' Running Tree said and led his pony off to graze.

'What was that all about?' Seth asked.

'It doesn't matter. Private joke.'

James put his arm round Sam's shoulders, she around his waist.

'Seems like you two are sittin' pretty,' Jacob observed with a wry grin on his face,

'Seems like we are,' replied Sam. 'Now, where's that coffee?'

James and Sam told them all about their journey. The tracking down of Burt, Sam's rescue. They had to skip over the bit about Running Tree avenging his two brother's deaths, even Sam had her eyes closed when Running Tree burst on to Burt.

'Seems like we all make a pretty good

team,' Lewis said with a broad grin.

'Seems like we do,' Seth replied. 'Even though you are jus' a kid.'

'I ain't no kid. I'm seventeen years old!' Lewis was quite indignant.

'Seventeen years old, eh. Well, I guess that don't qualify you for bein' called a kid,' Jacob joked.

They all laughed, except Lewis, as Running Tree returned.

'I leave now,' he said. 'Follow my brothers back to the Reservation.'

Sam was the first one to react.

'Do you have to leave?' she asked.

'No reason to stay,' was his reply.

'Well if you don't consider your friends here as good enough reason to stay . . .' James didn't finish the sentence.

'Sure seems like a shame for you to go off now,' Seth added.

'Might teach you how to like coffee,' James said.

'Don't go. Stay here with us.' Sam held on to both Running Tree's arms. He'd never been touched by a white woman before. He was embarrassed. 'Join up with us, please.'

Running Tree looked at each of them in turn. The thought of returning to the Reservation did not please him. He had no family there. These people seemed to like him. Treated him as an equal.

'I stay.'

Sam hugged him, the others slapped him on the back and shook his hand.

'Wanna try the coffee?' James asked.

'One thing at a time,' Running Tree replied.

They all laughed.

'Seems we got some plannin' to do, Seth an' me,' Jacob said. 'Gettin' too long in the tooth for this range-riding business. Not many cattle runs no more, trains take 'em mostly. Work's getting harder an' harder to find.'

' 'Sides, the ol' codger here ain't as supple as he used t' be, creaking bones o' his keeps me awake at night,' Seth added.

'There's got to be somethin' we can all chip into,' James said. 'That is, if you're planning to stay aroun' an' all.'

He looked towards Sam.

'Well, you may as well know, I'm very fond of you all, especially you, James. You know that. But I just can't see what you need me here for. I'm a city girl, really.'

'If'n you're a 'city girl' I'm a gonna take up bronco bustin' for a livin'.' Seth said and rocked with laughter.

'He's right. You ain't no 'city girl',' Jacob added.

'OK, maybe I'm not. But what do we do now?' she asked. She looked at them one by one, waiting for a response.

'Well,' James started. 'I sure would like to be with you, Sam.' He blushed brightly. 'Hell, I can't say none of what I want to say in front of them.'

'We know what you mean son,' Jacob said. 'An' speaking for myself, if'n I was fifty — no thirty years younger, you wouldn't get a look in.'

'Silver Bird.'

They all turned to look at Running Tree.

'What's that supposed to mean?' Seth asked him.

'You seen aeroplane before?' he asked.

'Well, no, not until Sam here dropped outta the skies.' Seth looked perplexed.

'Imagine not many people seen one either,' Running Tree said.

'Are you suggesting what I think you are?' asked Sam.

'Sure.'

'What the hell's he suggestin'?' Seth asked.

'You dang fool. Use the aeroplane there t' entertain folks,' Jacob said.

'Sure,' Lewis said, 'that way, we'd make a lot of money.'

'How'd you figure that out, son?' Seth asked.

'By charging people to come to our, er, what could we call it?' Sam asked.

'A circus?' Seth offered.

'A Flying Circus!' James added.

'Goddamn, if that ain't an idea to beat everythin',' Seth said, rising to his feet. 'Goddamn!'

'Silver Bird Flying Circus sure got a pretty ring to it,' James said.

'Well, we'd better get started then,'

225

Sam said. 'Because at the moment, I'm the only one who can fly.'

'You were about to take me up, Miss Sam,' Lewis said.

'Right you are, Lewis,' Sam replied. 'What are we waiting for then?'

'I'll tell you what we're waitin' for,' James said as he pulled her to her feet. 'We're waitin' for you to show *me* how to fly first, then Lewis. Then you'll be my wife.'

'Oh, James, of course. Yes, to both things.'

We do hope that you have enjoyed reading this large print book.

Did you know that all of our titles are available for purchase?

We publish a wide range of high quality large print books including:
**Romances, Mysteries, Classics
General Fiction
Non Fiction and Westerns**

Special interest titles available in large print are:
**The Little Oxford Dictionary
Music Book, Song Book
Hymn Book, Service Book**

Also available from us courtesy of Oxford University Press:
**Young Readers' Dictionary
(large print edition)
Young Readers' Thesaurus
(large print edition)**

For further information or a free brochure, please contact us at:
**Ulverscroft Large Print Books Ltd.,
The Green, Bradgate Road, Anstey,
Leicester, LE7 7FU, England.
Tel:** (00 44) **0116 236 4325
Fax:** (00 44) **0116 234 0205**

REMARQUE'S LAW

Will DuRey

Ben Joyner has no argument with the people who settled on the grassland near Pecos, but other cattlemen have long considered the range their own domain. Ben's boss Gus Remarque believes a dollar a day buys not only a man's labour, but his loyalty too. When that loyalty might involve killing or being killed, Ben wants to wash his hands of the dispute. So he quits the ranch and rides east. But then a strong-willed woman alters his plans . . .